Mackinac Triangle

Clint H. Dunshee

Mackinac Triangle

By Clint H. Dunshee
© 2016 Mackinac Triangle
Swartz Creek, MI 48473
Cover design by Clarissa Yeo

All rights reserved. No portion of this publication may be reproduced, stored in an electronic system, or transmitted in any form or by any means, electronic, mechanical, photocopy, recording, or otherwise, without the prior permission of Clint H. Dunshee. Brief quotations may be used in literary reviews.

Tell-Tale Publishing Group, LLC

Printed in United States of America

Dahlia Imprint

Author's Note

It is important for the reader to remember this is a work of fiction. Not everything in this story is true. Of course there is a Mackinac Island in Lake Huron. There are many shipwrecks in the Straits of Mackinac. There are also several stories about ghosts and ghost ships being sighted throughout the area. The area is rich in military history, and the Americans did occupy the fort at the time noted in the prologue.

However, there was no shipwreck of a vessel called the *Voyager*, no lost chest of gold coins, and no cursed treasure. There is no Great Lakes Research Lab on Mackinac Island. There is no "Mackinac Triangle," with unexplained disappearances of people, ships or planes in the area.

Dedicated to all the brave military people, past, present, and future, who serve the United States of America.

Prologue

Straits of Mackinac

(Convergence of Lakes Michigan and Huron, between the Upper and Lower Peninsulas of Michigan.)

May 25th, 1801

The thirty-foot military sailing ship *Voyager* glided through the calm seas of Lake Huron, on its way to Mackinac Island. It seemed a calm scene, but it was obvious to the ten soldiers on the ship that their commander, Captain Ross, was nervous. Of course, they were carrying the payroll for the fort, in gold coins. Pirates or local Indians would love to steal the gold. Even though the local Indians had no use for the money between themselves, they could use it to trade for valuable metal ware, blankets, rifles and salt.

Captain Ross took a long look through the hand-held telescope, and then lowered it with a sigh. He still didn't see anything, but it didn't make him feel any better. There was a fairly thick fog that night, and another ship could be on top of them before they realized it. The captain had wanted to delay taking the payroll to the fort by one night, to give the weather a chance to improve, but the commander of Fort Mackinac, Colonel Holmes, had overruled him on the issue. The fog would make it just as difficult for any thieves to see them, he reasoned.

"Pirates to our left!" yelled a young lookout named Lieutenant Teller. "And they've got Indians with them too!"

Cursing, Captain Ross ran to the rail to see another sailing ship approaching at high speed, along with two canoes full of

Iroquois Indians trailing just behind. It seemed obvious that they wouldn't be able to make the island before being overtaken.

"Break out the oars! Row, row!" ordered Captain Ross.

"We won't make it. They'll be on us in seconds," said Lieutenant Teller, who seemed strangely calm.

The captain knew he was right, but he also knew the pirates and Indians would never get the payroll. "Help me here, Lieutenant," ordered Captain Ross. They took the heavy chest and dragged it to the edge of the ship. Ross looked down at the water, and then glanced toward the island. They were in about twenty feet of water. They could dump the chest, wait for the danger to pass, and then return with men skilled in diving to recover it.

"Now, push!" Captain Ross and Lieutenant Teller dumped the chest overboard, opposite the side where the pirates and Indians approached, to block their action.

"We'll sail a bit longer, then sink this ship. They will think we sunk the coins with the boat, not where we actually did. When they are gone, we'll come back and recover the chest," announced Captain Ross.

"Very good sir, a cunning plan," agreed Teller.

"Have the men fire into the boat and sink her. I want the *Voyager* at the bottom. The men can swim to the island. We aren't that far off. I'll be the last to go. See to it now!"

"Right away, sir!"

Moments later the *Voyager* was on its way to the bottom, in about twenty feet of water. The men swam away while Captain Ross fired his musket and pistol at the attackers, trying to cover his men. When the last had gone, Lieutenant Teller jumped overboard and Captain Ross splashed right behind him. As he swam, Ross permitted himself a grateful smile to see his men making it to the island. Suddenly, intense pressure engulfed him. He was shoved forward, and he gasped for air. The gray water around him turned a dark red. Ross realized he had been shot in the back. His last thought was to wonder if he would remain conscious long enough to make it to shore.

He came to three hours later in the fort hospital. His groan sapped what little energy he could summon.

The fort doctor sat next to his bed and smiled. "Relax, you've had a busy night," he stated.

"The payroll. I must go recover it." The doctor gently laid a hand upon his shoulder.

"Calm yourself, Captain. Let me tell you what happened while you were unconscious, after one of your men pulled you to shore and got you to the hospital. While that was going on, a couple of your men saw Lieutenant Teller sneaking into a rowboat. He looked very suspicious, so they called for the shore patrol. They followed him and watched as he met up with the pirates who dove for the gold, right where the traitor told them it was located. The soldiers then attacked. The chest fell overboard again, but they managed to capture Lieutenant Teller alive.

"They got the traitor?"

"Yes. All of the pirates and most of the Indians were killed, but they got him. Colonel Holmes says the trial for treason will start whenever you feel up to presiding over it. Colonel Holmes figured that you deserved that honor, considering what you just went through."

"What about the payroll?" asked Captain Ross.

The doctor shook his head. "I'm afraid it's lost. The men figured it fell in about eighty or ninety feet of water, and it was getting dark, so they don't know the exact location. Although I know Colonel Holmes will have men dive for it, I'm afraid it's lost."

Captain Ross nodded. He felt profound shame at losing the chest and felt like he had let the men down. It wasn't something he'd ever really get over.

Three weeks later Captain Ross was recovered enough to preside over the trial of Lieutenant Teller. The disgruntled officer was quickly convicted of treason, and was sentenced to death by firing squad.

The men were assembled and Lieutenant Teller was placed in the center of the parade field where he refused the blindfold a young soldier held out. The rest of the fort population looked on, jeering him and throwing rotted fruits.

Captain Ross ordered it stopped and spoke to Lieutenant Teller. "Any last words, Lieutenant?"

Lieutenant Teller spat on the ground and remained defiant. "The army never paid me what I was worth. I had that gold coming to me! Nobody else will ever get it, either. I claim this gold, even in death. My curse on all those who would dare take it from me!"

"Enough! Never again will you betray your country," Ross declared. "And never again will you have the power to harm the truly brave and hard-working soldiers who actually did deserve that gold!" Turning to the men lined up to carry out the sentence, Ross cried out, "Ready! Aim! Fire!"

Shots rang forth. Lieutenant Teller's kneed buckled, and he fell to the ground, blood pooling around his head and torso.

Suddenly, the wind picked up and the waves on Lake Huron went from one foot to six feet as though the water had come to a raging boil. Soldiers near the shore gasped in fear and moved back from the lakeside toward the safety of the fort. The sentence had been carried out, but more than one attendant shuddered and remembered Lieutenant Teller's curse.

Chapter 1

Shells began to fall. Bullets laced the ground. Becky dove for cover while trying to help the wounded nurse. They got her on the litter. Tried to get away. Billy ran, how could he just run? He left them. He left her! Jack was hit and hit again, but bravely carried on. Jack died. Billy ran. The bullets continued to zing. The shells rained down. Becky killed a rebel, took a person's life away.

Becky bolted upright with a start. Her short hair was matted to her skull. Her pillows and blankets were soaked with sweat. Becky's chest ached, and she gasped for air. A look around the room confirmed she was safe at home in Detroit. Becky knew her parents were already very worried about her, so she decided not to tell them about this latest dream.

They wanted her to take up the military on their offers of counseling. But as much as Becky appreciated the military trying to help her through her PTSD, she respectfully said no. She would figure a way to go on with life herself. After all, it was her life, her choices, and her consequences.

Swinging her legs over the edge of her bed, she scuffed into the fuzzy slippers her mom gave her for Christmas and headed for the kitchen and the enticing aroma of coffee.

Before they left for work, her mom always reset the coffee maker, and her dad refolded the daily newspaper and left it on the kitchen table for her. She smiled at their thoughtfulness as she filled a big mug and took a seat at the table, separating the classified section.

Becky knew she needed a job, but realized she needed one that was somewhere quiet, somewhat easy, and without stress--at least until she could put the pieces of her life back together. She browsed past the usual dead-end hourly content, then saw an ad for summer employment on Mackinac Island. She had visited the island before and realized it fit the quiet and peaceful component she was looking for. Reading through the posting, she smiled. Not only was it a government facility, a lab of some kind, but there were several positions available. This could be the perfect opportunity for her.

Mackinac was a quiet island in Lake Huron, a huge tourist area. It would be a busy place, but not stressful at all. There were not even any cars on the island. People got around by walking, riding bikes or horses. Becky visited just before going into the Air Force. The homes there were quaint, Victorian architecture, and she seemed to recall fragrant lilacs in the spring. Yes, it was the perfect place to sooth her soul and ease her troubled mind.

* * *

Her initial application approved, she had now been summoned to Mackinaw City for an interview. There were various positions open, so Becky had no idea what job she might get. But at this point she didn't care. She'd clean up after the horses if it allowed her time to absorb some of the Island's tranquility.

Now it was just a waiting game for Becky, waiting for the door to open and someone to call her name. Becky reread the letter. Then she looked to the door where the interviewer was working. She hoped and prayed for the umpteenth time that she'd be accepted. It had been eight months since the incident in El Salvador, as the government had put it. Becky was still having trouble coping. She still had nightmares, still woke up sweating, thinking it was happening again. She saw Billy running away, abandoning her to an almost certain death, and then Jack dying and leaving a grieving wife and children. A month after it occurred she personally delivered the letter to his wife Tina in Carmel, California where they lived. It had been a tragic, tearful moment to say the least.

Tim read the letter again, and sighed. He had been instructed to show the letter for an interview in Mackinaw City for a position as security officer at some research facility on Mackinac Island. While he was encouraged about the prospects of getting a decent job, he still felt low. To fall from nearly becoming a state trooper to a security officer at some backwoods lab wasn't how he had seen his life going.

Well, beggars can't be choosers, he counseled himself, repeating the exact words his father had used. The more he thought about them, the more they stung. His mother strongly encouraged him to go, as did his father, although without the same encouragement. Tim figured he had little choice in the matter, and reminded himself he should be grateful that he might be close to getting a solid, respectable job. And if he did well at this, he could always try again to become a state trooper.

Tim took another look at the beautiful woman sitting next to him. She was reading what looked to be a similar letter. He decided to break the ice. "That letter looks familiar. You here for an interview too?"

Becky was surprised by the interruption. Irritated that her privacy was being invaded without her permission while she was trying to calm her nervousness, Becky turned to the voice next to her, ready to tell the guy in no uncertain terms to mind his own business. But when she saw the friendly eyes looking inquisitively at her, she paused. He was about her age, with dark wavy hair and big brown eyes. But the smile was what really entranced her. It was warm and inviting, and seemed genuine. She liked him at once, despite herself.

Then something in her mind snapped. The handsome visage of Billy Tompkins came flooding back. He had had a nice smile and pretty eyes too. Becky's Teflon shield slid up and she regained her frosty composure.

"Yes. I'm waiting to be called in."

"Me too. I'm Tim Green." Tim extended his hand to her.

Becky hesitated, but took the hand with just a hint of a smile. "Becky Vasquez."

"Pleasure to meet you, Becky." Tim continued to be friendly, outgoing.

Becky was determined to remain distant, but she could still be cordial. After all, she might end up having to work with the guy. Her tone softened just a hint. "You too, Tim."

"I hope you end up getting a job. Good luck," Tim said.

He seemed so sincere, Becky couldn't help but smile back.

The door they'd both been waiting for finally opened and a middle-aged man stepped out, holding some folders. "Becky Vasquez, Tim Green? Would you mind coming with me, please?"

The two got up and followed him to the room beyond. As they entered, they saw a long desk with a female sitting behind it. She seemed a little older than them, perhaps late twenties or early thirties. Her short blond hair was cut neatly at the base of her neck. She wore a warm, inviting smile. There were two chairs facing the table. Obviously they were for the two of them.

Remembering proper reporting protocols she'd learned in the military, out of habit Becky walked behind one of the chairs, and stood with her arms crossed behind her.

Tim was much more casual. He went straight to the other chair and took a seat. He cocked a curious eye at Becky, as she remained standing. The female seemed curious about this also, until the man reached down and pointed to something on the application in front of her, which caused the lady to nod.

The older man then became all business. "I am Archie Lames, and this is Sara Holmes. I am the director of the Great Lakes Research Lab on Mackinac Island. Sara is the head scientist. Ms. Vasquez, please be seated," said Archie, apparently unsurprised by her strict military bearing.

"Thank you, sir." Becky sat quietly.

"If I may point out, Ms. Vasquez, er…can I call you Becky?" asked Sara.

"Of course."

"You don't have to be quite so formal with us. You're not in the military anymore. What we do in the lab is very important and does require discipline, but we are much more relaxed. We want the employees to feel comfortable and at ease, literally as well as figuratively."

"Thank you, ma'am," said Becky with a lopsided grin. She noticed Tim giving her a curious look, but tried not to let him know she'd seen it.

"Now, we can get on with the process," said Archie. "Becky, you applied to an *open class* job on the island. Given your excellent military background we know you have great punctuality and leadership skills, and that you learned how to deal well with people when you worked as a medic. We've approved you for employment as a tour guide at the lab. It will mean guiding tourists through a working facility, providing information and answering questions while preventing them from disturbing other personnel. How do you feel about that?"

"That sounds just fine, sir. Thank you very much. I should point out though, that I'm hardly an expert on the Great Lakes. I understand that the research being done here concerns the Lakes."

"I like that honesty. It won't be a problem. Sara here will make sure you know all you need in that department."

"Thanks. I look forward to working with you, Ms. Holmes," said Becky.

"Call me Sara. It will be my pleasure to teach you anything you need to know".

"Now, Mr. Green. I see you made it through most of the training at the Michigan State Police in Lansing, but didn't make a minimum grade in the high-stress scenario portion, is that correct?" asked Archie.

Tim seemed embarrassed. His face turned pink and he looked slightly away from the twosome across the table. He glanced at Becky, and she could tell he was uncomfortable having the information revealed in her presence. She didn't blame him, but she couldn't help wonder if he was yet another coward who ran in the face of danger, leaving his team behind. She averted her attention, but was very interested in hearing his answer.

"It is true. I wanted to be completely transparent about what happened. Specifically, I made a couple mistakes, stupid ones I'm afraid, in the hands-on portion of the final exam. I shot a dog, an obvious friendly, and failed to move some vagrants to safety, away from the possible crime area. And-and though I got off a round and took down one of the armed perps, I was taken out by one of the drug dealers. Looking back, I know every wrong move I made, and if I had the chance to retake the test, I'm positive I would make the right choices. You don't need to worry about me running from danger, or not defending any of the staff should the need arise. I promise you that I would be able to do whatever was necessary to keep the facility and personnel safe if given the chance."

"I see. And now you feel you would be a good candidate as a security guard at the lab, correct?" asked Sara. Tim nodded quickly, still unable to look either of them directly in the eyes.

"Well, I thank you for your honesty. I think it's a very valuable asset in an employee. I won't hammer someone for making mistakes, as long as they are big enough to admit they made them." Archie glanced at Sara and said, "If you agree, I think we have filled our last two positions."

Sara nodded, and said, "Okay, it's settled. Congratulations, you're both hired. You two will be working together, which is one of the reasons we interviewed you in a team setting. It gives you a chance to get to know each other just a little ahead of time." She paused and took a quick drink of water, then went on. "Now, on your way out we'll arrange housing for you, probably in Mackinaw City, though I know most employees prefer the island. With all the summer employees flooding the area the rooms fill up fast. If you end up in Mackinaw City, you'll get a year's pass to take the ferryboats to and from the island."

"Congratulations to both of you," Archie said, standing. The rest of them stood and shook hands.

"We'll see you in two weeks for orientation, and the actual season opens one week later. See you both then," said Sara.

Becky smiled her thanks, and turned to leave the room. She was so relieved to have gotten the job, she hadn't had time to mull over Tim's response to his high-stress scenario failure. When he touched her arm to get her attention, she pulled away and looked up at him without speaking.

"So it looks like we'll be working together."

She nodded, but didn't respond.

He glanced away, clearly uncomfortable, then cleared his throat and said, "Are you okay with that?"

Becky knew exactly what he meant, but wasn't sure herself how she felt about it yet. She shrugged and said, "Are you okay with it?"

"If you mean do I think I can handle the job, then yes, yes I do, or I wouldn't have taken it. If you mean am I okay working with you, then yes again. In fact I'm looking forward to getting to know you better." He smiled then, a full-cheek, all-the-way-to-his-eyes smile.

She responded to his simple honesty, despite herself, and returned his smile. But remembering the reason she had nearly been killed and the too easy way she had been fooled by another boyish grin, she pushed him away mentally, nodded, and said, "I guess I'll be seeing you in a couple weeks, Tim."

Turning, she walked away.

Chapter 2

Grand Hotel Ballroom
Mackinac Island
May 1, 2013

Nautical Observations as reported from the Great Lakes Research Lab on Mackinac Island. Lake Huron: Waves 2-3 feet, water temperature 48 F, air temperature 58 F.

Tim had been at the lab all week, training and orienting to the new job, and it had gone well. His direct supervisor, Steve Grant, was awesome. Things really seemed to be turning around for him. When he was offered a bonus to check invitations and make sure nobody tried to crash a large wedding at the Grand Hotel, he jumped at the chance.   Only registered and invited guests were allowed on its' premises, and the hotel wasn't about to have its strictly enforced policy tarnished by a large event. Tim was more than happy to help them hold their record.

He looked around, trying to spot Becky Vasquez. She had been invited to the wedding. He knew that, because Archie Lamas wanted her to get some publicity out about the lab. Apparently she was public relations for the lab, not just a tour guide.

During the first week at work he'd found himself more and more attracted to her romantically, though it had been a one-sided interest to this point. She was polite, but treated him no differently than any of the other employees. He was hoping that in a more social environment he would have more luck getting her to relax. So far, he hadn't had the opportunity to ask her out.

Finally, he spotted her and moved to say hello.

Becky felt like she'd been doing well at the reception, getting the word out about the important work the lab was doing to ensure the Great Lakes would be around for a long time and remain a pure source of fresh water for future generations. She smiled at the new bride and groom, Tom and Jenny Lake. "Welcome to Mackinac Island. I hope you are finding it peaceful and romantic."

"I love it here," enthused Jenny. "You must too, since you work here."

Becky chuckled at her excitement. She hoped the pretty bride had found a real man who could actually be relied on, which she herself doubted actually existed. If Billy couldn't be trusted…no, she wouldn't go there. Not here, not now. These two were happy and deserved some encouragement. "Yes I do too. It's a major reason I came to work here. I wanted a job that's quiet and laid back, not to mention it just happens to be beautiful here," responded Becky.

"Well, you couldn't pick a better place then. We've got a house in Mackinaw City, and a cottage on Rock Island. We plan to split our time at both places," said Tom.

Becky felt someone touch her shoulder and turned her head slightly. It was Tim. She had to force herself not to look directly into those friendly, outgoing eyes. Something about Tim made her feel at ease. He seemed genuinely friendly. He had dropped several casual hints about going out, but thus far Becky had ignored those hints, quickly changing the subject. She wasn't going to let Tim or any man cause her pain ever again. Still, she found her resolve slipping the better she got to know him. He was handsome, easygoing and friendly. He had faults, but being a coward was not one of them. It took bravery to own up to having made poor decisions when in high-stress situations as honestly as he had. He didn't have to tell the reason he never became a state trooper. It was a choice, which meant not all of his choices were bad, either.

"Well, Tim, no party crashers I assume," said Tom as a way of greeting him.

"Nope, no problems at all. I just wanted to come by and offer my congratulations to the both of you. I understand you're taking off soon?"

Jenny looked at her watch. "In fact in about thirty minutes. We're taking our boat to Rock Island. It's about ten miles west of the bridge, on the Lake Michigan side of course. We bought it cheap last year when the state auctioned some of those islands off. It's only about a forty-acre island, but it is beautiful. We have a getaway cabin there complete with dock and a nice-sized beach we had made. Well, I'm going to change. I'm anxious to go. There's nothing like a boat ride with an almost full moon." Jenny excused herself and hurried off.

"Mr. Grant says to keep the boat under eighty. Guess you have a fast one huh?" asked Tim.

Tom nodded with a wide grin. "Yes, it can haul ass alright. But I'm an old lady when I drive it. I love that boat, so don't worry about me pushing her too hard. Well, if you'll excuse me, I'm going to say goodbye to our guests and get changed myself."

"So, how's it going?" Becky and Tim turned to see Steve Grant approach them.

"Very well, sir. All is quiet. Everyone seems to be having a good time," reported Tim. Steve nodded.

"I'll take over now. Why don't you two youngsters take a little walk. I hear it's really nice down the steps toward the Grand's gigantic pool."

Tim and Becky looked at each other and shrugged. "Sure. Thanks, boss," said Tim, just a hint of a smile on his face.

Becky and Tim turned away, heading toward the pool. At first they walked along in an awkward silence. Becky looked anywhere but at Tim.

Tim finally decided it was time to break the silence. "Look Becky, how about lunch tomorrow? Please?" he blurted.

She hesitated, and he held his breath.

"Okay, I'll give in, lunch tomorrow," she finally said.

Relieved, he let out his breath. He wasn't about to let her know how surprised he was. He was too grateful.

They arrived at the pool a few minutes later. It was indeed very impressive. It was larger than Olympic size, and the shape of an hourglass. It even had a fountain in the center. A few people were actually swimming in it, despite a slight chill in the twilight air. Others mingled around the area.

Tim pointed, and they took a seat on one of the couches surrounding the pool.

"So how did you like the Air Force?" asked Tim casually.

Becky shrugged. "I liked it fine. I just decided not to stay in for various reasons." She stopped speaking and bit her lip, looking away. She had a sudden pained expression on her face. Tim felt a sense of dismay. Obviously it was a painful topic to her that he shouldn't bring up. He needed to try and quickly rectify that.

"Sorry, I didn't mean to pry. I know how things don't always go the way we plan. I thought I'd be a state policeman by now and look what I'm doing. Not that there's anything wrong with it. This is a nice job," said Tim.

Becky's opinion of Tim raised a notch or two. "Do you plan to try again?" asked Becky bluntly.

Tim looked acutely uncomfortable, then looked away. "Can we talk about it another time? I'm just not ready to talk about it yet."

Becky shrugged. "Sure, no problem."

"Thanks."

"Well, I really should head back to Mackinaw City, I'm taking the seven-forty-five ferry. I'd better run if I want to catch it."

Tim nodded. "I'll walk you to the dock. You know, make sure you stay safe and all. It's getting dark outside. Even though violent stuff like that never has happened on the island before. You never know."

Becky's face suddenly turned sour, and Tim realized immediately he'd said something wrong. When she jumped to her feet, he did the same.

"You think I need you, or any man to protect me? Timmy, I should be protecting you." With a couple quick arm strokes Tim was on his back with Becky on top of him, one hand on his throat, the other in a half fist, ready to smash his face."

Tim gasped in amazement, and then burst out laughing.

"What's so funny?" Becky demanded, scowling.

"I haven't been put in my place quite like that before. I got the message loud and clear. Tell you what, I'll walk with you to the dock for the fun of it and you can protect me."

Becky released her grip, and slowly got off him. Her face went from deadly serious to confused and then she even sported a small grin. Rising to her feet, she said, "Wow, I'm sorry. I overreacted. What you said, it just hit me the wrong way." Reaching out her hand, she helped him to his feet.

"You'll have to tell me about it someday, but don't worry about it right now. Maybe you can teach me some of that stuff one day," said Tim, rubbing his neck. Glancing around, he put his hands up and said, "No worries. We were just goofing around."

Suddenly realizing where they were and what she'd done, Becky noticed the curious stares of the people around them and felt her cheeks burning. She shrugged sheepishly and turned to hurry away, with Tim close on her heels. "I can't believe I just did that. Let's get to the dock now," she whispered.

Thirty minutes later the Lakes had said all their goodbyes, and walked to the dock and boarded their sleek, red and black sea cruiser. They were happy, jubilant. They had a bright future ahead of them. They laughed, hugged and kissed, as they got onboard.

"Whoa there…save some for Rock Island," said Jenny with a devilish grin.

"Hmmm…maybe I will go more than eighty then," laughed Tom. They were still laughing as they pulled out into the Straits of Mackinac.

There was no other boating traffic, just a ferry rapidly shrinking in the distance, heading to Mackinaw City. The water was turning a deep, dark blue as night crept over the waters. It was a beautiful but ghostly sight. Jenny shivered slightly and pressed closer to Tom, who smiled and put his free arm around her. The five-mile-long Mackinac Bridge, Mighty Mac to the locals, came into view as they sped toward it. Jenny slowly pulled away from Tom and was peering intently forward, squinting in the distance.

"Do you see that?" she asked.

"What? Nothing but water out there."

"Over there, to the left a little. It looks like something black, like a big shadow. It looks like something is rising out of the water."

Tom eased back on the throttle and peered in that direction. For the first time he could see something. It was like she said, a large grayish-blue shadow. It seemed to come out of the water and then hover a few feet above it. It became to loom larger, and larger. Tom realized why. It was getting closer to them. Coming straight for them. A feeling of doom came over Tom, a sense that the shadow was evil. The instruments began to die, one by one. The compass spun crazily, like someone held a magnet to it. The bluish haze turned to a glow, and seemed to change shape. It was human-like, and then expanded to be almost twenty feet high.

"Tom, get us out of here…please!" Jenny sounded frantic.

"Yeah, I think you're right." Tom gunned the throttle and thankfully the engine responded and they sped away. He didn't know how fast they were going since the speedometer was stuck on zero for some reason, but as long as they got away from the shadow thing he didn't care how fast they went.

"Faster, faster!" Jenny was hysterical now.

Tom spared a look behind. The shadow was only about fifty feet behind them now and gaining. No matter how fast he went, it easily keep pace. It changed form, and become suddenly even more human-like. He could almost make out facial features. Arm-like appendages extended and reached for the boat.

Tom pulled out the radio and switched to the emergency frequency. "Mayday, mayday, mayday. Island marina, Coast Guard this is the Lake boat cruiser, seven eight nine M I. Something is after us. Help, it is nearly on us!"

There was a brief pause, and the Coast Guard came on. "Lake cruiser this is the Coast Guard Station in St. Ignace. What is your location? Repeat, give us your location! What is after you? Over."

"It's too late! It's already here!"

"What is it, what is there?" Nothing but static followed. The Coast Guard radio operator tried several times, but got no answer.

The commander turned toward a junior member. "Get a cutter out, ready for search and rescue." The man nodded and hurried off.

On Mackinac Island they listened to the exchange. The radio operator seemed to shiver at the terror in the voices. Whatever it was that had been after them, well, must not have been anything ordinary. The harbormaster knew the Coast Guard would send a boat out, but also figured they could use all the help they could get. He rounded up three volunteers and they headed in the dark waters of the Straits. The two boats crisscrossed the area for six hours, seeing nothing. The search was called off with the intent they would start again at first light.

Chapter 3

Mackinaw City

Becky sat up quickly, her gaze darting around, her breathing fast. She could again feel sweat stinging her eyes and rolling down her face. She closed her eyes as she sat in bed and tried to force herself to calm down. She was safe in her apartment in Mackinaw City. In an hour she'd be on a ferry to the island, and the official first day of work. Good, very good. She needed to start work. It would help her put those memories of El Salvador behind her.

She cleaned up quickly and walked to the ferry dock, bumping into Tim as she arrived. He was his usual cheerful self. Becky tried to take in his happiness and pleasant demeanor, thinking it would be good for her. But she found herself remaining mostly detached from him as they boarded the ferry and began the fifteen-minute trip to the island. It took her a while to let the dreams go sometimes.

Tim somehow sensed something was up and quieted down, instead content to look out the porthole at the passing waters. She appreciated his ability to sense when she needed to be alone with her thoughts.

* * *

The large boat cruised under the Mackinac Bridge and headed east toward nearby Round Island, which was basically a next door neighbor to Mackinac Island. There were ten young people on the boat, all barely twenty-one or twenty two. They had been on the boat partying all night, except the two people piloting the boat. While the others were below deck sleeping it off, they cruised the boat toward the island.

"Check that out," the taller pilot, Chuck, pointed left, toward Mackinac Island. His present copilot, Todd, looked to see a boat drifting. It didn't seem to have an anchor down, and there were no visible boaters.

"Pull up next to it. Something is wrong here. It looks like someone just left the boat to drift. That's weird," said Todd. Chuck pulled up next to the boat and the twosome attached lines to hold it against their large yacht. It was a beautiful speedboat of the sea cruiser class. Black and red stripes made it look even classier.

They boarded the boat and looked around. Nothing, nobody was there. The keys were still in the ignition, everything was still in order, nothing spilled or in disarray.

"Maybe they are scuba-diving?" asked Chuck. Todd shook his head.

"If that were the case they'd have a dive flag out. Plus they'd have the anchor dropped. It's like they left the boat in a real big hurry," said Chuck.

"Say, there's a small cabin underneath," announced Todd. They slid down the ladder and looked around. The bed was made, and again all was in good condition.

"I don't like this. Let's call the coast guard," said Todd. With a nod, Chuck agreed.

The Coast Guard Cutter pulled up next to the red and black boat owned by the Lakes. After tying up to the boat the commander sent two persons aboard. One looked below deck the other on top. Both of them seemed to have a sense of dread that something bad had happened here, though they could find no evidence to support their feelings.

There was a safe below deck that wasn't touched. There was money and valuable jewelry found, undisturbed though in plain sight. Nothing had been disturbed. The Lakes had clearly stated that they were being chased by something. But what would chase them and then not take the valuables when they caught them? And catching them was another thing. This was a very fast boat. Your average cruiser out there wouldn't be able to come close to catching them.

The commander didn't like this one bit. Something just wasn't right. And to make matters worse, his men were beginning to get a little jumpy. Something about the boat made them all uneasy. The commander knew he needed to attach the boat to the cutter and tow it back to the station, but he was uneasy about that too. He didn't like the way this incident seemed to be affecting his men. Though he had given the standard line there was no such thing as the Mackinac Triangle, he was beginning to wonder.

Something was going on in these waters. Not all of it could be that people were not paying attention while they were boating. He couldn't help but think that some of the stories of ghost ships and apparitions around the area might be true. He shivered despite himself, then quickly caught himself. He couldn't let the men see him like that.

They were military professionals and were expected to act that way at all times while on duty. And whether there was a triangle or curse didn't matter. He had a mission to accomplish. And no matter what happened, no matter how weird things seemed to get, no matter how creeped out he and his men got, that mission *would* be accomplished.

* * *

As Becky and Tim arrived on the island they turned in tickets to a local bike rental that would provide them with bikes for the entire summer season. Bikes were the fastest and easiest way to get around the island.

As they arrived at the lab, they were surprised to see a buzz of activity. Archie Lamas, Sara Holmes and Steven Grant, Tim's boss were speaking with a coast guard officer. Another coast guard member hurried in and spoke to the commander. All of them wore grim expressions. Commander Oslo nodded, spoke briefly to Archie, Steven and Sara, and hurried out the door.

"What's up?" asked Tim.

"Another disappearance. The young couple, the Lakes are missing. It's strange though. They couldn't find anything last night, no trace of the boat or the couple. Then this morning a yacht finds the boat drifting near the bridge. They had crisscrossed that area a half dozen times last night. They should have spotted it. Damn I hate islands and water!" complained Steven.

"Foul play? They were rich. Maybe they were robbed? I hate to say it I really liked the Lakes. But maybe they were robbed and killed, and the bodies dumped. After all, bodies never wash up in the Great Lakes," offered Becky.

Archie shook his head. "The boat was in perfect condition. They had valuables on board, and none were touched. Anyway, it they were robbed, they would have taken the boat too," pointed out Archie.

"It's like the boat was gone last night, and just popped back on the water. Looks like another triangle and curse victim to me," said Steven.

"That's enough of that talk! I admit this is something of a strange occurrence.   It just doesn't fit the profile of a standard robbery. But that's not our problem here. Our job is to study these waters not enforce laws on them. Today this area starts the summer season and tourists will be piling through the area. The last thing we want to do is scare them off by talking about a curse that's causing our own version of the Bermuda Triangle," said Archie sternly.

Tim snapped his fingers and looked thoughtful. "Yeah, I remember the story. It was that traitor Lieutenant Teller on board the *Voyager* right?" asked Tim.

Sara nodded. "Yes. The story was he made a deal with Indians and pirates to steal a payroll of gold coins.   They captured Teller alive, but the chest was lost in deep water."

"So what happened to that bastard Teller?" Becky asked. Her sudden anger caused Sara to stop and stare at her in surprise.

Tim cocked his head and looked at her curiously, trying to figure out what about the story had really set her off.

When Becky didn't explain her agitation, Sara continued, "Teller was given a trial and convicted of treason in about three days. Later he was sentenced to death by firing squad. His last words were used to curse the gold and all who tried to find it. Rumor has it that he also cursed the entire Straits, and his ghost sometimes appears and causes ships to mysteriously vanish."

"Wow…so you think there's really a curse?" asked Tim. Sara shook her head.

"No, I don't really think so, but…" she shrugged. "But who knows for sure?"

"But ships go through the area all the time without vanishing, look at all the ferry boats and the trips they take every day," pointed out Becky.

"True, very true. But it's about those other few, about a rate of five or six per year that vanish without a trace. Or like last night, the boat and people vanish, then the boat reappears, but no persons are ever found. I sure believe in it," said Steve.

"So Teller kind of picks and chooses what boats and people he makes vanish?" asked Tim.

"If you believe in the curse, yes. But I tend to think he concentrates on boats that happen to venture over where the chest is, or in his mind are just too close to his gold," said Sara.

"Has the gold ever been found?" asked Becky.

Sara shook her head. "No, it hasn't. Scuba divers with underwater metal detectors have looked for many years and never found anything. We get *a lot* of divers looking every year too. Today the gold coins would be worth about twenty million dollars."

"Geeze! No wonder a lot look. I may be looking myself," laughed Tim.

"Okay people, listen up. It's time to open, and for the scientists to get to work. I don't want to hear any talk of curses and this so-called triangle stuff. We have real, serious work to do, so let's get to it. Vasquez, if people ask about it, just give the company line, there's no curse, no mysterious disappearances. Just a lot of green people making errors in boating."

Becky just shrugged it off.

The research lab opened a few minutes later and a group of fifteen tourists were waiting. Becky greeted them and got enthusiastic greetings in return. "Please remember this is a real, working lab. The scientists are doing serious work here. Please do not talk to or approach any of them. I'll approach them for any questions I cannot answer. Now, if you would all follow me please."

Becky showed the group around the lab, explaining to them all that was being done there. Finally at the end of the tour came the time for questions. A man showed her a newspaper headline already talking about the disappearance of the Lakes.

"How do the scientists account for that? he asked.

"There are many possible explanations. Perhaps one of them got sick, or dizzy and fell overboard. Then when the other tried to save their partner, the other panicked, pulling them both under. And of course, as you may know it is not unusual for bodies not to be found in the Great Lakes following accidents," said Becky.

"The paper says it could be another case caused by the Mackinac Triangle, where ships and people disappear like the Bermuda Triangle," said the man. Becky shook her head.

"We here at the lab, don't believe…"

An elderly woman who spoke up cut her off. "The paper also said something about others believe these disappearances are caused by the Teller curse, what is that all about?"

Becky spoke of the story of the lost gold coins.

"So we can go look for this gold legally? asked a younger man.

"Yes of course,' responded Becky.

"Excuse me." The man suddenly bolted from the lab. He got amused looks from the others as he practically fell over himself leaving.

"Wonder what he's going to do?" stated one of the group, while the others laughed.

Becky answered a few more questions and the group left the lab.

She did two more groups before lunch and was glad when it was time to eat. Although she kept her promise to Tim about having lunch with him, she kept telling herself it wasn't a date.

The twosome rode their bikes to an area a block to the north of Main Street, to a restaurant called the Islander Diner. They sat and ordered.

Tim knew Becky was carrying baggage and suspected it was from her military service. She hadn't wanted to talk about it before, but he hoped she would open up about it. He began cautiously, not wanting to make her angry again. "So, you did four years in the Air Force, is that why you act kinda… official?"

Becky shot a wary eye at him.

"I suppose that's a big part of it. You had to act with a certain level of courtesy and a good dose of discipline. You needed to have a certain sense of urgency in all you did. You were expected to always go above and beyond in wearing the uniform and doing your work. They never wanted anyone to settle for minimum standards. Those that did were severely disciplined and looked down upon, know what I'm saying?"

Tim nodded. "I think I do. When I went to the police academy it was a lot like that. I always tried to set high standards and always excel. I tried to make myself the best state police candidate there."

Becky sat back in the booth and tried to size him up some more. She felt something of a kinship with him. He seemed genuine to her, not fake at all. Tim might actually be like this inside too, which she was finding she hoped was true. Ah, but Billy had that sort of effect on her too. And look how that turned out. *Don't let your guard down, girl. You'll just get burned again.*

"So, why are you here? Why aren't you driving one of those blue cars around? You haven't given up have you?" asked Becky.

"I…can I tell you later?" Tim suddenly looked acutely uncomfortable. Becky raised her eyebrows in surprise. This was the first time she has seen Tim seem unhappy. She'd clearly inadvertently struck a nerve. For just a second she was glad someone else had baggage they were carrying around besides her. But then she couldn't help but feel somewhat guilty. "Of course we can talk about that later, when you feel up to it."

At that moment the food gratefully arrived.

"Thank you, Becky, I appreciate that."

Becky shrugged as if it were no consequence. "We all have some things in the past we'd rather not think about, things that cause us pain. And sometimes you need to get to know someone before you trust them with such information," said Becky, her expression suddenly turning hard like steel.

"I agree, completely," responded Tim. "In fact, what do you say we spend the day Saturday doing the tourist thing? We are off work. Let's spend the day doing the island together. Then if you have a good time with me, perhaps we can try to get rich and go dive for the lost gold of the *Voyager.*"

"How did you know I was a scuba diver?" asked Becky.

"I heard you telling Sara."

"Tell you what, Saturday is a date. We'll explore the Island together. But as far as after that, we'll see how that day goes before I decide whether I want to do more things together. Fair enough?"

Tim smiled broadly. "Fair enough."

Chapter 4

Mackinaw City

"An hour? You're nuts!" exploded the tallest of the twosome, named Carl Ellison.

"Mr. Ellison, if you just…"

"Listen and listen good," explained the second man, Thomas Steele. "We are both CEO's of major downstate Michigan firms, and we make more money in a month then you will in a lifetime. We get what we want, when we want it. Do you understand?"

"Now just a minute…" began the youngster, but was cut off again, this time by the arrival of a second man, the harbormaster of the marina, Ronald Thurrow.

"What's the problem here?" he demanded sternly.

"Very simple, we want gas now, not an hour from now," demanded Ellison.

"That's right, so don't make us wait," added Steele.

The harbormaster sighed. "Listen sirs, I truly wish I could just snap my fingers and make gas appear out of nowhere, but we are at the mercy of the delivery truck." Both of the men looked like they were about to explode, when a gas truck pulled into the marina. All the men looked out the window at the sound of the semi. "Lucky for you, I must have snapped my fingers," murmured Steele. "We really are used to better service. Now, are you all competent enough to fill our sub with gas?" asked Steele with an annoying air.

Thurrow shrugged, and pointed to a sign, it read, "ALL GAS SELF SERVE, PAY BEFORE FUELING."

"No way! I do not pump my own gas!" thundered Ellison. Again Thurrow shrugged, and motioned for the youngster to leave the immediate area.

"I'll tell you what, I'm going to fuel your sub just so I can get you two out of here, so you don't disturb the other boaters, how's that?" remarked Thurrow.

"Fine," replied Ellison, looking smug.

With the utmost haste, Thurrow fueled the sub, shaking his head the entire time.

After ten minutes, the sub was fueled, and the men towed it back to the marina to their large yacht, which was about the size of one of the ferries that provided service to Mackinac Island. After getting the sub attached to the yacht, they made a trip to a local dive shop to get a dive flag.

The young lady ringing up the purchase decided to be proactive and offer more to the two men. "Do you need any dive gear, wet suits…"

She was promptly cut off by Steele. We don't scuba dive. That's for common people. We are using a submarine."

"I see, well what if you get a breech or something? Being down in the sub without being a diver could be very dangerous."

"Like your opinion has been asked. Just do what you're told and no more. Geez you people in northern Michigan are rednecks. I'm surprised you all use indoor plumbing and utensils," stated Ellison flatly.

"Sir I wasn't trying to tell you what to do. I just was suggesting that being in a sub without dive gear could be very dangerous. What if…" she was promptly cut off by Steele.

"Like my friend said, just ring up our purchase and mind your own business. We know what we need, and no local moron tells us anything." After that remark the men left the shop, getting a hand gesture from the young lady as they left.

The two men boarded their luxurious yacht, and towed the sub to an area of about one hundred feet of water. It was west of Mackinac Island, and east of the Mackinac Bridge.

Neither Steele nor Ellison cared about the *Voyager* or what happened to it. All they wanted was to find the lost payroll of gold coins. Both of the men chuckled at the part of the story that told about Lieutenant Teller's curse on the treasure.

"Okay, this is as good a place as any to begin. Let's get the sub in the water and make ourselves another twenty million," laughed Steele.

"You bet, let's go!" agreed Ellison. They placed the dive flag in the water, and then boarded the sub. Then Steele released the cables holding the sub to the yacht.

Ellison took his normal position at the controls, and made sure all gauges were in the green. Steele's job as copilot was to be another pair of eyes to search for the treasure. Since he made slightly more money than his friend, he figured that it wasn't his job to do the piloting of the sub.

It wouldn't be long now, Steele mused, and another twenty million dollars would be added to their coffers. A few minutes from now they would find the chest with the gold coins, grab on to it with the sub's robotic arm, and haul it back to the yacht. It would be the easiest money they ever made.

"Okay, down we go," announced Ellison. Slowly, the sub began a shallow dive into the blue waters of Lake Huron. The visibility was about fifteen feet today, not bad at all. That would help with the visual search for the chest. Ellison watched the depth gauge hit twenty feet, and then he leveled the sub off. The sonar was active now, and he used it to plot a course toward

Mackinac Island. A few salmon flashed by, surprised by the sudden iron intruder. A Northern Pike came closer, bolder than the salmon, its sharp teeth clearly visible to Ellison as it nipped at the metal before swimming off, apparently satisfied the sub was no threat to it.

"Like a little shark," Ellison mused to himself.

"What's our depth now?" asked Steele, interrupting his thoughts.

"Oh, let's see, twenty-five feet. We are in the area of the wreck," announced Ellison.

"Slow down. I don't want to miss the chest because you were speeding, that's twenty million dollars out there," said Steele.

Keeping his eyes on the instruments, Ellison slowed the sub down. Gradually the wreck of the *Voyager* came into view. The depth gauge showed twenty-three feet. It was in very good shape, a good object for common scuba divers to descend to.

It looked almost ghostly in the pale green water. It appeared to be tilted slightly on its side, and larger concentrations of fish seemed to congregate around it. The wooden planks were mostly in good shape, thought a few had rotted over the years.

The wreck was getting too eerie for Ellison, and he steered away, toward the west. He began a slow, gradual decent to deeper water. The water was a light green, then a navy blue, then almost black. The depth gauge needle swung to higher numbers, reading deeper and deeper. They saw a sandy bottom come into view at ninety-five feet.

Suddenly the sonar picked up an object to the left of the wreck, at a slightly shallower depth. Ellison turned the sub to the new object, trying not to get too excited, for it could easily be a pile of rocks or something.

"Steele…" began Ellison, but was cut off.

"Yes I see it. Let's see, it appears to be in eighty-eighty of water, shallower than it was reported to have been. It is two and one half feet long and eighteen inches wide, and eighteen inches tall, with a three inch arch in the center," informed Steele, his voice rising with excitement.

Ellison noticed this. "Calm down my friend, let's get closer and get the flood light on it," cautioned Ellison. Steele relaxed, knowing his friend was correct as usual.   Ellison in the meantime had snapped on the front floodlights. The powerful lights cut through the dark waters, and a few minutes later showed a vague outline of the object. Whatever it was, it was partially embedded in the lake bottom. It seemed like part of the left side was missing, like it had rotted partially. As Ellison maneuvered the sub closer, the front lamps confirmed it was the chest.

"It's the chest alright," said Ellison, his voice shaking slightly.

"What's the condition of it?" asked Steele. Ellison took a closer look, and placed the front scope on a higher magnification.

"Looks pretty good. The left side is partially decomposed, but not too bad. The coins in it are heavy, and should still be inside the chest. We'll probably lose a few pulling the chest in, but not too many." Steele nodded.

"Okay. Get the arm working and pull the chest in. I don't like us being under the water too long. It gives me the creeps."

Steele had barely gotten the words out when Ellison began to operate the sub's robotic arm.   As Steele watched Ellison operate the arm, he became vaguely aware of a bluish, gray haze, floating outside his porthole. Steele was shocked to see it looked like a person, a smiling person. Then it abruptly vanished.

"Did you just see," began Steele.

"Yes, I saw it, looked like a person, or a ghost." Now Steele began to laugh.

"Okay, that's enough. We're just getting scared because of the curse and the so-called Mackinac Triangle. Our brains are telling us there are things out there that really aren't."

"Well, just the same, why don't we just leave the chest and get out of here? We are both rich enough. This is too creepy." Steele shook his head.

"You can never be rich enough. There is twenty million in gold out there. Just grab the damn chest, pull it in, and then we'll get out of here."

With great reluctance, Ellison went back to work using the arm. Skillfully, he had the arm latch onto one of the handles of the chest. He then began to retract it, and the chest was reeled slowly to the body of the sub.

Without warning, a bluish-gray glow filled the sub. The ghost-like figure had returned.

"Shit, I'm out of here!" yelled Ellison. Now, even Steele agreed.

"Okay, I--" He never got a chance to finish the statement. Bolts mysteriously unscrewed themselves and shot around the sub, water squirting in.

"Hurry up, you fool! Get us out of here!" Steele was shouting now. Ellison tried to release the chest, but it stayed attached to the arm. Seeing it wouldn't work, Ellison manipulated the controls to climb back to the surface. They would escape whatever the hell that blue thing was, and still get the chest. The sub raised a few feet, and then leveled off. No matter what Ellison tried, the sub just floated, dead at thirty-five feet.

"Get us out of here!" Steele shouted again.

"I can't. There's no response to the controls! All the instruments just died at once. That's not possible!" Steele turned pale white, as did Ellison. The sub was rupturing everywhere now, and water was pouring in. In a matter of seconds they could barely keep their head above water.

"We have…to…swim for it," said Ellison between gasps.

"I don't know…how…I-I-I…" stammered Steele. Ellison shook his head.

"Just hold your breath and float to the surface, exhale as you go, slowly, blow out little bubbles as you get closer to the surface," said Ellison. He pushed his way through a large hole that had ruptured in the side of the sub. He began to swim to the surface.

Steele took as deep a breath as he could, and pulled his way through the ruptured sub. As he floated to the surface, he slowly let the air out of his mouth while blowing out small bubbles of air as he did so.

In the meantime, Ellison kicked as hard as he could to the surface, now just about fifteen feet away. He only hoped after he surfaced that he wasn't too far from the yacht. He was dead tired from the swimming and knew he wouldn't be able to swim a great distance once he got to the surface. He was less then ten feet from the surface, when the bluish form returned. Ellison looked in horror as it came directly at him. It looked very human, but like a ghost. It was smiling. One of its arms reached out in snake-like manner and coils wrapped around his chest. The squeezing became unbearable, and then incredibly, it stopped. Ellison saw the unmistakable form of a boat bow park itself directly above him. A second later he rose to the surface, and was gratified to see Steele surface next to him.

"Here, grab the line!" Ellison turned to see a young man on the boat throw a lifeline to them. They grabbed on and were pulled out of the water, onto the man's small sailboat. Steele looked around and spotted their yacht floating about a hundred yards away.

"That's our boat over there," he pointed to the large yacht.

"Thank you very much, you saved our lives. I'm Carl Ellison. This is Thomas Steele, and you are?"

"Tompkins, Billy Tompkins. I have a friend who works on the island, at that new science lab. I want to pay her a visit. And also, I kinda owe her, since she kicked and punched me in the face. I figure I got the right to return those to her."

"Why the hell would she do that?" asked Ellison. Billy relayed the story about what had happened in El Salvador.

"That's crazy, everyone has a right to protect their own life first and foremost. We are on your side. Why don't you spend the summer with us? You can help us find the treasure and make sure nobody finds it ahead of us. We'll give you ten percent of whatever the treasure is worth," said Steele.

"Sounds good. But what if someone else should find it ahead of us?" asked Billy. Ellison got an evil grin.

"We'll make sure that it is us who ends up with it. If someone does the work and gets it for us, all the better. The most important thing is that we are the ones who end up with it in the end."

* * *

The chest was engulfed by the bluish, nearly human form, which somehow attached it to a hook at the bottom of a nearby buoy. The haze slowly lost its human appearance, and faded down to the deep depths of Lake Huron.

* * *

Not far away, on Mackinac Island, Becky stifled a yawn. She saw the group grow to about fifteen people outside the lab, fudgies as the locals called the seasonal visitors to the Island. She ran her hand through her hair, absently noting that it was growing out and would soon brush her shoulders.

Deciding she would wait just five more minutes to let any stragglers catch up, she glanced around the lab. She loved working here and had interacted enough with the staff to decide she might have found her future career. She would love to be a real scientist here--not just a guide for tourists who thought the Great Lakes were salt water. She once even had a young blonde ask how often they had shark attacks in the Great Lakes.

But, she had to admit that she was happy here even as a guide. The island, the job were working for her. Coming here had provided the therapy she'd hoped.

Glancing at her watch, she walked toward the door. Hearing an exclamation, she glanced to her right and noticed some extreme readout spikes on one of the computers that gave a constant update on the water conditions of Lakes Huron and Michigan. Her friend Sara Holmes was pointing at the screen and shaking her head in disbelief.

She hurried over and asked, "What's up Sara?"

"Oh, hi Becky. The impossible just happened on Lake Huron." She pointed to an electronic map of the lake. "This area of Lake Huron just had the water temperature rise from forty-eight degrees to sixty-five in a split second. The waves went from two to six feet at the exact same time. And it was just in Lake Huron. Lake Michigan didn't change. It lasted about five minutes, and then suddenly went back to normal. It's just impossible." Sara again shook her head in disbelief.

Becky leaned forward for a closer look at the screen when a hand on her shoulder pulled her back. She snapped around ready to jerk away when she saw it was the director of the lab, Archie Lamas.

"Leave the analysis to the real scientists, Vasquez. The tourists are waiting," he said sternly, pointing to the ever-growing group of people. Becky's cheeks burned, but she said nothing. Nodding an affirmation, she glanced at Sara.

Sara smiled slightly, and gave her an "I'm sorry about that jerk," smile. Becky smiled back, and headed off to the waiting group of tourists.

"So what is so important?" demanded Archie. Sara showed him the data.

"Buoy zero three five is reporting these readings."

He waved it off, totally unimpressed.

"So? All this proves is that the buoy in that area is malfunctioning. Look how this weather and conditions only occurred at this particular area of the lake. Tomorrow I'll have one of our security people take a boat out there and bring the buoy in. We'll get it fixed." Sara nodded. She had to admit that she didn't have any other reasonable explanation for the sudden change in conditions. It seemed that Lames was right, that this was just the work of a malfunctioning buoy.

In the meantime, Becky had properly greeted the tourists. A couple of elderly females complained she'd made them wait too long, but Becky ignored the remarks, stating that she had to assist one of the scientists.

"Remember this is a working lab. Please do not disturb the people working here. I'll show you the entire lab and be happy to explain what they're doing."

Twenty minutes later she had done just that. Despite her frequent amusement and occasional shock at the lack of knowledge and misinformation the visitors possessed, and her longing to be a real scientist, she enjoyed her job. Except for the two old women who complained, she received thanks for the nice tour. She smiled sweetly, and said goodbye to them.

"You mask your true feelings very well."

Becky turned to see the source of the remark. This time her smile was genuine, despite herself. It was Tim.

"Glad I play my role well," she laughed.

Tim shrugged. "I know some tourists drive you crazy, but they do pay the bills. And despite the fact that they are often hilarious, you manage to make them feel their questions are legitimate and that you take them all very seriously."

"Can't argue with that logic," she laughed.

Tim grinned. His boss Mr. Grant always made him laugh. At the moment he was kicking up a fuss with the director of the lab, Mr. Lamas. He threw up his hands in anger, while Tim strained to hear what was being said. Finally Sara spoke to him. Whatever she said worked, as he visibly calmed down. He walked over to where Tim had been talking to Becky. Becky excused herself and walked away. It appeared that Steve wanted to talk to Tim without her listening in.

"Sometimes I hate being head of security here. Every time they have something that has to be done, we have to do it whether it has anything to do with security or not. Like the big shots here can't do something that might make them sweat or blow their hair out of place!"

"So what have they got you doing?"

"I have to go out in the morning and pick up some damned buoy that is malfunctioning. Don't they have techs for that?"

Tim wrinkled his brow. "So what's so bad about that? Sounds like fun to me."

"I hate the water! And those butt heads know it! I'm scared of the water. I'll get eaten by some triangle ghost or some mutant shark."

Tim laughed so hard he got a cramp. He straightened up before speaking. "You better relax boss. You're not so young anymore. You'll give yourself a heart attack. Besides there's no ghosts in the Great Lakes. No sharks either."

"I said mutant sharks, ones that can survive in fresh water. They have actually found some of those. But I know I better relax," mumbled Steve.

"Tell you what, why don't I go and get the buoy for you? I don't mind."

The older man shook his head. "No thanks. I'll do it. I ain't gonna let them know I'm scared of water and sea monsters."

Tim laughed again. "Okay boss, have it your way."

* * *

The young couple was having a great time water skiing. The boy gunned the engine of the boat and looked back as his girlfriend got a determined look on her face to actually get up on

44

her skis this time. Though she was new to the sport, she was getting better at it. She wasn't ready for jumps and stuff, but she was better at the high speeds and sharps turns.

Her boyfriend looked back and saw the confident smile, and knew it was time to boost that confidence even more. He gunned the engine and performed a sharp turn. She responded by hanging on with almost grim determination. Her skis seemed to graze each other slightly, one went over the top of the other. She was immediately thrown forward, while her skis peeled off her feet and flew up in different directions. She let go of the rope while her body kept moving forward, hydroplaning over the two-foot waves.

When she finally came to a stop, she shook her head, trying to clear the cobwebs. She didn't have a floatation device on, and she wasn't very good at treading water either. She spotted the nearby buoy, and gratefully swam to it, holding on. She saw her boyfriend begin a slow arc with the boat, returning to her. She waved her left arm, making sure she held on to the buoy with her right. She sighed; she'd never live this little incident down.

As the boat inched closer, something like fog seemed to rise out of the water, off to the left of the boat. Then it seemed to change color, from a whitish to gray, to a dull blue. It was a strange fog though. It drifted into an almost human shape. As she watched it several seconds, it went straight for the boat, and was now very human like. Its arms reached out to grab the boat. The young lady had never seen anything like this before, but whatever it was, it wasn't good. She began screaming a warning.

"Look out! Look out Jon!" She pointed to the left. Jon turned and saw the form for the first time. He barely had time to gasp in astonishment before the form enveloped him and the boat. Then, a second later, both were gone.

The young lady was past being hysterical now, she wasn't that sane. The haze began to float her way now, with the large arms reaching toward her. She pushed herself away from the buoy, and swam toward the nearest land she saw, Mackinac Island, though she doubted she'd make it. It was a good half-mile away, and she wasn't a strong swimmer. Several quick glances behind her revealed the haze hovering over the buoy for just a moment, and then it disappeared. She breathed a quick sigh of relief. She continued to swim for the island. Her joy quickly turned to terror as the haze emerged to her right, and headed for her again.

"No!" She wailed, intermixed with sobs. Then she heard a different sound, the unmistakable drone of a boat. It was coming directly toward her. She waved her arms in frantic haste, screaming for help. The haze disappeared again, this time sinking below the water.

Steve Grant was still pissed about having to go out on the water when he saw the person in the water, screaming for help. He turned the boat slightly and sped in the direction. As he stopped the boat, the young lady began clawing at the boat, trying to get in.

"Easy, easy, it's okay. Let me help you." Steve pulled the lady on board, surprised by her hysterical rambling.

"Do you see it? Is it here? Did you see it? The mist, or bluish haze? Is it gone?" she asked frantically, burying her head and trying to hide on the floor of the boat. Steve glanced around.

"No, just blue skies."

"We-we…n-need…l-leave…hur-hur-hurry…" The young lady stuttered now, and began to shake. She appeared to be going into shock.

Steve saw the buoy, just a few yards away. He had to hurry. This lady was in trouble. He picked her up and laid her on the back seat. It didn't escape his notice how she clutched tightly onto him. He pulled her hands off and wrapped her in a blanket.

"Try to relax, everything is fine now. I'll have you to the island in a few minutes." Steve pulled up next to the buoy and pulled it alongside the boat and attached it. Then he hurried back to the island, calling ahead to make sure medical people would be waiting at the dock when he arrived.

The medical people were at the dock in an automotive ambulance, only one of two automobiles allowed on the island. They quickly began to access her, determining she was going into shock. A state policeman was there also, ready to escort them back to the island clinic. They determined that this was something that didn't need to be transported to the mainland, and that they could handle this situation.

Archie Lamas approached Steve as the ambulance pulled away with the young lady.

"I assume you brought the buoy in, after all, that is what you were supposed to do."

"Yeah, yeah it's attached to the boat. And what was I supposed to do, just let her drown out there?" said an exasperated Steve.

"I didn't say that, and I'd watch your tone, it's sounding rather insubordinate," warned Archie.

"Listen I--" Steve was cut off, as a state policeman and the coast guard Commander Oslo approached him.

"Mr. Lamas, we need to talk, *now*." He looked around and saw Sara, Becky and Tim helping Steven get the buoy off the boat.

"Have your other people join us too. This is important. *Very important*," said Commander Oslo. The state policeman wore a grim expression.

"The lab is opening in thirty minutes--" began Archie.

"Delay it one hour," insisted the Commander. "And before we begin, get the data from that buoy. I need to know what's up."

"It may have malfunctioned, that's why we were bringing it in," added Sara, approaching the group.

"How soon can you know?"

"I'll get it to the lab and open it up, then run through its internal checks to see if it malfunctioned or not. If it didn't I'll have the data out in fifteen minutes. If it did malfunction then all the data will be corrupted," said Sara. Commander Oslo nodded.

"See to it now, we'll be in Mr. Lamas's office waiting. Mr. Grant, and Mr. Green, please join us."

"Okay." With little time to spare the foursome hurried the buoy to the lab.

Becky watched with envy as Sara quickly opened the control panel on the buoy and ran through its internal checks. Fifteen minutes later, the checks confirmed it was working perfectly. She then downloaded the stored data and photographs that were stored inside. Ten minutes later she pulled out the data and quickly reviewed it. Sara scanned the photos and her mouth dropped open. She felt a chill run up her spine.

"What is it?" asked Becky, noting her reaction. Sara handed her the photos. It was a series of ten photo's showing the water skiing young woman fall, and then the boat arriving near the buoy to pick her up. It also showed a fog-like mist approach the boat the closer it got to the buoy, where the young lady was hanging on. The mist seemed to change shape, and was soon looking like a thirty-foot tall person with arms reaching to the boat. The arms picked up the boat and its driver, then in the next two photos both the boat and driver were gone. Only empty water, with suddenly larger waves present.

"Holy crap. We better get to the boss's office now," remarked Sara.

Becky nodded her agreement.

Commander Oslo looked at the photos and data and sighed. This wasn't good, and they all had major damage control to do now. He tossed a local newspaper on the desk, the headline boldly proclaiming, MACKINAC TRIANGLE CLAIMS ANOTHER VICTIM. Just below that, *Did the Curse of the Voyager Treasure come into play?*

"How did they find out so soon?" asked Archie.

"The news people always have those police and military scanners on. They heard the mayday call by the driver of that boat, and the response by us," said Commander Oslo.

Sara and Becky entered the room, and Sara threw the photographs on the desk.

"What is that? It doesn't look like regular fog to me, more like some monstrous human," began Steve.

"That's enough! This is just a weird looking fog, that's it! Just like clouds that sometimes take on funny shapes. I don't want to hear any talk of curses and disappearing people and boats in the triangle. Vasquez, you're bound to get a lot of questions. Those tourists coming in will have seen this story. I expect you to stifle it. We don't need our bread and butter scared off," said Archie sternly. Becky nodded. Commander Oslo looked troubled.

"I sure would like to know what the hell is going on. But anyway, I need to run. I have to go find this submarine and those rich owners. I'll count on you all to keep this as low key as possible."

Becky looked confident. "Senior Airman Vasquez at your disposal Commander. I'll perform this duty to the best of my ability."

Commander Oslo looked at her with an approving eye. "Ah, a fellow veteran huh? That is good, very good. I know now that the job will get done. I'm counting on you Airman Vasquez to keep things as business as usual as possible, while we try to sort this out."

"Yes, sir," replied Becky in an official manner.

Tim smiled inwardly at the exchange. He was increasingly curious about Becky. Though she certainly seemed proud of her service, there was something else there too, something causing her regret, anger. He wasn't a professional by any means, but she almost acted like she had PTSD. There was some trauma in her background, and that was certain. The cause was something he hoped to find out in the coming days. It hadn't been easy to get her to even consider going out with him. It seemed to Tim that perhaps a man had done her wrong in the recent past, probably a military person also. Though he was dying to know what it was, he knew he'd need to be patient. When she was ready she'd open up to him.

Becky knew what Tim was thinking. He wanted to know where her distrust of men came from, and why she didn't like to talk about her military service, but she'd tell him about it in her own time, if at all.

Becky hadn't really decided what to tell him, if anything. Tomorrow they were going to spend the day together, and perhaps depending on how the conversations went, she might open up to him. But why should she at all? He was a man and though she might be able to become friends with him, she could never really trust him.

Becky found her resistance to him becoming more and more fragile as she spent time with him. Her avoid him at all costs had become a willingness to be friends, but nothing more. And yet, there was just something about Tim that screamed at her to trust him. He was nothing like Billy. Even her feelings were different this time. Tim was every bit as handsome as Billy, but there was much more substance underneath.

If only he didn't possess the one fatal flaw she just couldn't accept, the inability to engage his intellect and training in dangerous situations. He was a man who couldn't be counted on when needed the most. Her first impression had been right, she reminded herself, Tim couldn't be trusted no matter how nice he seemed.

Chapter 5

Nautical Observations as reported by the Great Lakes
Research Lab on Mackinac Island: Lake Huron: Water
temperature 52 F, Waves three to four feet, Air temperature 65F.

The coast guard cutter sliced through the water, toward the wreckage that was visible in the distance. They were investigating the call from some big shots about their sub getting wrecked while exploring the depths of Lake Huron. The commander of the cutter wanted to get this over with. The men seemed to have the same feelings of dread with this rescue they had with the finding of the Lake's boat. It was as if something was different, like something evil was at work. The commander maintained the strictest discipline, and that was what allowed his men to continue to function normally.

"Sir, over to the left, wreckage from the vessel," said a crewman, pointing as he looked through the binoculars. The commander turned his attention to the left and saw what looked like a metal fish, wounded. But the commander knew the fish-like shape was part of the privately owned submarine.

"Send a boat over to the sub, and bring her to the cutter, let's determine what happened to it," ordered the Commander.

"Yes, sir." As the boat was being launched, two divers from the cutter surfaced, and swam over to be hauled into the ship.

"Anything?" asked the commander. The diver pulled his mask down.

"A lot of wreckage, pieces. There is one side of the sub almost intact. I've attached the line to it, so you can bring it in.

We might be able to figure out what happened with that large section."

"Okay, do it. Then let's get it towed back to station."

The men in the cutter wasted little time in complying. They just wanted to be gone from this scene, the sooner the better.

* * *

The newest group of tourists grew to twenty before Becky decided it was large enough for this particular tour. She preferred that to be the maximum size. It just made things easier on her and the scientists trying to work. It wasn't a very large building and large groups could be disruptive. Becky stood back out of the way as Tim checked each person, making sure there were no forbidden items or weapons on any of the persons. It probably wasn't a necessary task, but one never knew these days. All it would take would be one nut job to cause a major problem. Tim grunted in satisfaction and nodded to Becky that she could begin.

"Welcome to the Great Lakes Research Lab. Please remember this is a working lab. So stay close and don't stray. Or my friend Tim over there will get upset." The group laughed as Tim smiled and winked with a quick wave.

"Now I'll begin."

"Sorry to interrupt, ma'am, but look at this."

Becky was cut off immediately by the topic she knew she'd face today. She pretended to be interested in the woman's newspaper clipping.

"And this isn't the first time," the woman continued. "What do you have to say about this? Is it another victim? Is there a curse?"

An elderly man handed her another newspaper with the story of the missing water skier and boat. Becky sighed. "Okay, let me tell you all a story that occurred in 1801." Becky relayed the events that occurred that fateful day. The tourists' mouths seemed to hang open as she spoke of the events. There seemed to be more genuine interest in the story than another information she ever provided about the lab's actual function. "So, in conclusion, some people think the disappearances in the area are due to the curse placed on the gold coins by the traitor Teller."

"What's the official view?" asked a tourist

"That there is no curse. Yes the events occurred of course, and yes that bastard Teller said he would curse the area, but that's all nonsense, are no such things as curses or ghosts. As for the disappearances, it could be a combination of things, accidents, boater error, rogue waves, even water spouts, and just plain bad navigation."

"I'm Thomas Steele. This is Carl Ellison. We are CEO's from major downstate firms. All you're saying is hogwash. It's pure lies! We had a sub wrecked due to the ghost of Teller. He's out there. Look for the gold and you will disappear for good."

Becky cleared her throat and asked politely, "If what you claim is true, then why are you both still in this dimension?"

Steele sneered. "I'm glad you asked. We were rescued at the last second. Guess our rescuer scared the whatever-it-was away. In fact, I think you know him. Come up here." he said, motioning to someone behind him.

Both Steele and Ellison smiled broadly as the young man stepped forward. Becky's mouth gaped open in shock. It was Billy, Billy freaking Tompkins! He had a wide smile on his face, mocking her sudden anger.

"Surprised to see me? Aren't you gonna give your old friend a hug at least?"

This couldn't be happening. Becky swallowed, unsure what to say or how to proceed.   Thankfully her military training kicked in and rather than bursting into tears of anger and rage, she said, "I believe I left you with the exact impression I was hoping for."

But even her military training couldn't save her for long. If only she'd been prepared. How did he dare show his face here? She had to get out of here. She wasn't ready for this. She began to feel tears sting her eyes.

"Excuse me all," she said, her voice soft and tightly controlled. The others in the group looked at her curiously as she walked over to a fellow employee, speaking briefly to him.

He shrugged and nodded.

Becky disappeared out a side door.

Steve walked over to Tim and whispered something to him. Tim nodded and followed the route Becky had just taken. The security chief walked over to the tourists with an inviting smile on his face. "Hello. I'm Steve Grant, normally head of security. But as Ms. Vasquez isn't feeling well, I'll take over the group. If you'll all follow me."

Tim had watched the display and was troubled by it. Obviously this was someone Becky knew in the military. Tim thought it likely he had something to do with her tight-lipped policy on her service, even her determination to keep him at arms' length. But what troubled him the most was the way she had run off. She was always so tough, strong and in charge of things. It bothered him to see her suddenly lose her composure so badly. Tim was glad Mr. Grant told him to follow her.

Whatever was up, Becky might need his help. Hopefully, she'd take it.

Becky fisted her hands. How could he be here? Why would he be here? And what in hell was he doing with those rich bastards? Becky didn't like this feeling of being out of control. Her hands were shaking as she walked, and she clutched them tightly together to try and stop them.

Betrayal, self-doubt, rage, Becky was feeling them all at once. She thought of Jack, and tears welled up in her eyes. Jack was dead because of that bastard Billy. She had thought she loved Billy, was even dumb enough to plan on sleeping with him after that mission had been completed in El Salvador. He had told her he loved her, and she had believed him. He had so easily left Jack, herself, Ashley and Diana White to die.

"Hey, you okay?" Becky turned to see Tim approach her, concern in his eyes.

"Yeah. I was surprised to see that guy." Becky closed her eyes and tried to keep herself focused so she wouldn't lose it again.

"Can you tell me?"

Tim was cut off as Billy arrived with Steele and Ellison in tow. He seemed to be buoyed with confidence as they flanked him on both sides.

"So how have you been, Becky?" asked Billy.

"Shouldn't you be in prison?" retorted Becky, her own confidence fueled by her growing anger.

"I did my six months in Leavenworth. I was a model prisoner, so now I'm out."

"So why are you here? You can't be looking for me," said Becky.

"Actually, I was. We didn't end our relationship well and I wanted a chance to make things right."

"You're being serious?" asked Becky incredulously.

"Of course I am. Now that I've partnered with these fellas, we will soon find that gold, and with my share I'll be rich. We could have it all. Come on, you're not still angry with me, are you?"

Becky was so shocked by his arrogance, she couldn't think what to say. She just stared at him, and was grateful when Tim interjected, "Everything okay here, Becky?"

"Actually these people are bothering me, Tim. If you'd send them on their way I'd appreciate it."

Billy looked genuinely surprised. "You need help sending us away? The Becky I knew a few years ago wouldn't need any help from any man for anything. I never really got over the surprise attack and those blows you managed to land on me because I was unprepared. It wasn't very nice."

"I think you three should leave," said Tim quietly.

Steele stepped forward. "Or what, rent-a-cop? You're just a dumb loser who couldn't make it as a real cop, in the real world, so you had to take whatever job you could get," said Steele, while Ellison and Billy laughed jovially.

Tim could feel his courage begin to evaporate. It was hard to argue with the truth. When things came push to shove, he got flustered and messed up. That was why he had failed the dangerous scenario exam when he'd been trying to make it with the state police.

"I uh, well, yes, it's time for you to go," he stammered over his words but managed to maintain his resolve and refused to back away from the older, well-dressed executive.

"This guard is responsible for the safety of all persons who work at the lab, and I clearly heard him tell you all to leave." They turned to see Mr. Grant.

Steele shrugged. They were drawing too much attention and it was obvious even to him that this newcomer wasn't about to be intimidated.

"Okay, no problem. We were just saying hello anyway." The three walked away.

Steven watched them go and made sure they were actually leaving, then he turned to Becky and Tim, a stern look on his face and in his tone as he spoke to Tim.

"Tim, come with me. Let's talk in private." Tim gulped, and nodded. Moments later they were in his office.

"You can't let those kind of comments bother you, Tim. Regardless of how or why you took this job, the fact is you took it. That means you are responsible for Becky's safety at all times, is that understood?" Tim felt remorse at his lack of confidence and the way the three men had nearly backed him down. He felt embarrassed that apparently Steve had noticed his hesitation.

"Yes, sir," he said, looking Steve in the eye.

"Good. You and Becky can both take the rest of the day off. You're shift is almost over anyway."

As Tim walked out of the office, he looked for and quickly found Becky. He found it more difficult to look into her eyes.

"Are you okay?" he asked.

Becky smiled. "I'm fine, Tim. Thanks for helping me out."

Tim rolled his eyes. "I blew it there, I--"

"Showed you were human, but recovered swiftly. I saw your discomfort when that arrogant bastard challenged you. He's used to getting what he wants by intimidating people. It's obvious.

But what is equally obvious is that you forced yourself to push back your self-doubt and stand your ground. I honestly don't know what I would have done without your help," finished Becky.

"Really? Well thanks. Who was that Billy guy anyway? Why did he upset you so much?" asked Tim.

"Tell you what, tomorrow I'll tell you everything. I just wasn't expecting to see him again. It caught me off guard. But tomorrow I'll explain everything, I promise."

Tim nodded.

"Tomorrow I will explain things to you too."

* * *

Owen and Sam sat in a boat in the calm water of Lake Huron as night began to creep over the vast waterway. Sam looked around nervously, straining to see in the darkness. He was sweating, and no amount of rubbing his hands on his clothing could stop it. His friend was intent on watching the fish finder, which he was using to find the chest of gold coins. They were in the tour at the lab when they heard the rich people tell how they were so close to finding the gold and decided to try to find it before the rich people came back.

"What about all those disappearances? And that curse on the gold? They must be connected. Did you not listen to *that* part of the story Owen?"

Owen shrugged. "Yeah, Sam, I heard that part too. But consider this, they could have just said that to keep people away, to scare them off from looking for the gold."

Sam looked unconvinced. "Then why didn't they take the chest? They said they found it. Then the curse thingy or ghostly thing came after them. They had to leave before it made *them* disappear."

Owen shook his head. "It's just a scare tactic. Look, they found the chest like they said. Then the sub suffers a malfunction, its hull got breached. More than likely due to shoddy workmanship. They *had* to abandon the chest or they would have drowned. So they cook up the story to scare others away. You see since there are so many stories about the curse and the disappearances, they knew people would believe them."

"But why mention it at all? Why not just keep it quiet?"

"It would have been a big news story, a private sub owned by fancy CEO's sinking. They knew people would find out they were looking for the gold. So they needed to try to keep others away. So they hatched the story. I for one don't believe in curses or ghosts. But I do believe in gold. And those rich dudes have enough money, so it's time to spread the wealth around. This gold is our ticket out of the daily grind that we are forever stuck in."

Sam sighed, Owen had clearly made up his mind and there would be no changing it now. He had to admit even he thought it was worth it to go after the chest. Curse or no curse he too wanted to desperately get out of the daily grind that barely makes a person enough to stay just behind in life.

"Looks like something on the fish finder that ain't a fish, about two feet long, seems to be at about seventy feet. Could be the chest," said Owen.

"As open water divers we aren't supposed to go deeper than sixty feet,' said Sam.

"For that amount of gold, I'll go the extra ten feet. We'll be fine. We have plenty of air and lots of time. We'll just take our time going down, and we'll stop every ten feet on the way back up."

"We've never done a night dive either, things are going to be very dark down there in daylight, but at night…"

"Relax dude. That's what these floods are for. We'll be fine. Now get suited up."

Sam could only sigh again at this point. There wasn't any turning back now. Owen was determined to go down, and that was the bottom line. No way would he let him go down alone, which he would do.

A few moments later they were suited up. Owen tested the floodlight and was satisfied it was working properly.

"Let's do it! We are going to be rich soon!" he crowed.

They leapt into the cold water and began the slow decent. By the time they were down fifteen feet, it was completely black. Owen snapped on the floodlight and the underwater world was revealed for the first time. Several fish, startled by the sudden burst of light, swam away at a brisk pace. A few actually came closer to investigate this unnatural occurrence.

For the most part, Owen and Sam ignored the fish. They were totally intent in finding the chest, if that indeed was what they had seen on the fish finder. They slowed, cleared their ears and continued to dive deeper; they were now at sixty feet, which was supposed to be the maximum depth they dove at their current skill level. But they didn't figure another ten feet would matter, not when you were talking about a few million in gold just a few feet away.

Sam saw it first, the vague outline of the chest. He tugged excitedly at the arm of Owen and pointed. Owen nodded and motioned for him to keep going. The floodlight clearly showed the chest now. It appeared that part of the wood had decomposed slightly, but it otherwise seemed in good condition. As Sam reached over, he was able to open the chest. It appeared the lock that had been on was for some reason missing. While part of one side of the wood had indeed decomposed, the rest was still intact. Most of the chest was still full of the gold coins. Owen was alongside him just staring into the chest.

Then, with a great jerk Owen was pulled backward. Sam turned around and his eyes popped at the sight. It was like a bluish gray fog or mist or maybe a cloud. But it looked like a large person, at least twenty feet high. Its arms seemed to be crushing the life out of Owen, who was struggling futilely to get away. The last thing Owen saw was what appeared to be evil eyes on the figure squinting at him. He saw bright white light surround himself, and suddenly all was dark.

Sam forgot everything, Owen, the gold, and his own personal safety. He knew nothing but pure terror. His body responded by soiling itself. He began kicking furiously to the surface, forgetting all about safety stops. At thirty feet from the surface, his mouth began to fill with blood and his body convulsed and jerked as nitrogen built up rapidly. He lost consciousness and began to drift limply to the surface.

The ghostly figure had yet again protected its gold and the arms pulled the chest away to another location. Satisfied the gold was again safe, the shape seemed to melt away, becoming one with the water.

* * *

Todd and Chuck were again piloting the yacht full of partying young people just the minimum age to drink, but old enough. There were fifteen people on the boat now, five more than when they had found the boat drifting. They were the only two who weren't drinking any alcohol again. The others were dancing, drinking, living it up. One of the more sober ones noticed a shape floating in the water and motioned for the pilot to slow the boat and turn to his port side.

"Geeze! That's a person. Call a Mayday medical emergency!" said Chuck. Todd wasted no time in complying, while Chuck leapt into the cold water and pulled the person onboard.

"What do you think?" asked Todd

"Looks like he surfaced too quickly. He's got the bends. He's gonna need a decompression chamber pretty quickly if he's going to live. I'll update the rescue people. Begin rescue breathing on him."

The others in the boat looked curiously at the events, and watched the Coast Guard cutter arrive. They would have the victim to shore in a few minutes and a jet helicopter would then rush him to the nearest decompression chamber in Marquette. Commander Oslo came aboard the yacht to question the two rescuers.

"You guys make it a habit of finding bad news, I guess," said the commander. Todd smiled wryly.

"I guess we haven't brightened your days much lately have we?" asked Chuck.

"You didn't find anyone else? There should have been one more person. Nobody dives alone, especially toward evening."

The kid who jumped into the water shook his head.

"That's true Commander, we are all divers too. But we didn't find anyone else. It's like the other person just vanished. Maybe it's another triangle mystery."

The commander frowned at this as his radio came to life. The divers' boat had been found. It was properly flying a dive flag, and was anchored. There were valuables onboard and nothing seemed to be disturbed. The boat was in good and seaworthy condition. They found two wallets and drivers' licenses identifying two persons. One of them was clearly the person who had gotten the bends.

"Well, thanks for all your help, I must get back to my duties." The commander and his men left the boat and boarded the cutter and sped off.

"What do you think?" asked one of the young people.

"I think the Mackinac Triangle has struck again." A third person, barely still sober joined the twosome.

"If it's there or not, we can't do anything about it. Come on, let's party!"

Chapter 6

Becky sat up in bed suddenly, her heart pounding, her face again drenched in sweat. She looked around the room, not moving from the spot in the bed, and let out a relaxing sigh. It was okay. She wasn't in that jungle again, she was safely in her room in Mackinaw City. She glanced at her watch. It was nearly seven. She and Tim wanted to start early that day and spend it seeing as much of the island as possible.

Becky slid out of the bed and showered quickly, putting on a polo shirt and shorts. It was expected to be nearly eighty-five that day so she wanted to be as comfy as possible. She slapped some sunscreen on her face and put on her Detroit Tigers baseball hat and looked in the mirror and grinned. *You're not that bad looking actually. Tim will like the way you look,* she told herself. Then she wondered why she even cared if he did. Was Tim beginning to break through the barrier around her heart? *No, I'm not falling for him. I'm just being polite and hanging out with a friend, that's all,* she told herself. Everyone needed friends, though she had to admit she wasn't doing a good job of convincing herself.

Becky smiled and nodded her head. She was back. The next time Billy popped in on her she'd most likely pop him one up side his head. She wasn't prepared emotionally to see him yesterday. It was just a total shock to her. But now she was fully back in charge of herself, and ready to handle anything he threw at her.

Her thoughts were interrupted by a knock at her door.

"Hi, am I too early?" asked Tim, cheerfully.

"No, not at all, let's go and see if we can explore the island without being swarmed by a bunch of fudgies," responded Becky.

"But you're from downstate."

"But I'm official now, so it doesn't count," she laughed. "Let's go."

Moments later they were climbing aboard the ferry and speeding to the island. Though they did this every day to get to work, it was different this time. Today they would actually be able to enjoy the island and do whatever they wanted, whenever they wanted.

"So, you going to tell me about Billy? What's the story there? I've never seen you look so unsure of yourself before," said Tim, picking his words carefully.

"I'm fine now, and I am totally back in control. He caught me by surprise; he was the last person I expected to see. But it won't happen again. He noses around in my business too much he's gonna get more of what he got in El Salvador. As far as what happened between us, I'll tell you later on today."

Tim nodded. "And I'll explain some things to you too. I didn't exactly shine on that confrontation with them yesterday."

They arrived at the island fifteen minutes later, and went to a nearby bike rental.

Becky and Tim decided to take the tougher route. They'd head up Fort Hill Road, and go through the center of the island. The island was eight miles around its perimeter, and mostly level, with a few steep grades. Of course the views of the water and the other nearby islands were nothing short of spectacular. Going through the center one would end up at the halfway point of the island on the perimeter ride, the British Landing site when they invaded the island during the War of 1812. It was three miles through the center, then four once the perimeter road was begun. But it was nearly uphill the entire first half of the ride, and very demanding, which is why it was part of the course for an annual foot race called the Great Turtle Trail Run.

The twosome were soon feeling the effects of the early portion of the ride. They huffed long before they reached the top. Just when it seemed inevitable that they would have to dismount and push, they reached the top of the hill.

Tim stopped, threw a leg over his bike and bent over next to it, sucking in air. Becky was out of breath too, but managed to laugh at his theatrics. It appeared she was in much better physical condition.

"Okay, iron lady, where to?" joked Tim once he had caught his breath. Becky pointed up a small trail.

"We go up this trail, and take the steps up to Fort Holmes."

Tim groaned. "Steps. Of course. Okay," he mumbled without enthusiasm.

Becky just laughed and led the way. Fortunately the trail was short, and the steps weren't that hard of a climb. And once they got to the top, the view was more than worth it. They could see for miles in many directions. They could see whitecaps rolling on Lake Huron far below, in fact over a thousand feet below. They could see nearby Round and Bois Blanc Islands. Then they turned their attention to Fort Holmes. There wasn't anything left inside, just grass now, with the outside walls still intact.

Becky stepped outside the fort and looked at the walls. She seemed to get a faraway look on her face. Her stare was blank, expressionless. Tim hesitated, and then approached her with caution. He touched her arm gently.

"You okay, Becky?" he asked quietly. Becky inhaled a gulp of air and smiled. She turned to Tim.

"Yes, I'm fine. I was just connecting to the American soldiers that were once stationed here. This was a very tense place for them. From this vantage point they were responsible for heading off a surprise attack on the main fort."

"Uh what do you mean, by connecting with them? How do you know they felt tense here?"

"Let me try to explain. As a civilian you might have trouble figuring out where I'm coming from."

"But you're a civilian now too," objected Tim.

Becky shook her head. "Only half at most. When you serve in the military, even after you leave, the military stays with you, so you're never really a civilian anymore. You're part of a fraternity, a family. That family is my brothers and sisters that have served in the military since the first shot at Lexington in 1775, right up to current conflicts, and the people currently serving. We are a tight group, and I can feel their presence, actually almost talk to them and get a sense of how they feel."

Tim looked from the fort to Becky, as if accessing what she'd just said. What she'd just stated had never occurred to him before. It was very profound, and Tim believed every word she'd just said. That faraway look on her face, it had been like she was in a different place and time. He smiled inwardly. There was much more to Becky then met the eye. She had it seemed, a very complicated personality.

"Come on, let's ride on," suggested Becky. They made their way down the steps and back to the waiting bikes. The next place they saw was the halfway point in the center of the island. From here on, it would all be downhill till they got to the road around the perimeter of the island.

About five minutes later they came to the site of the biggest battle ever on Mackinac Island. It had occurred in 1813, during the War of 1812. The Americans were attempting to recapture Fort Mackinac after a surprise attack by the British had captured it a year earlier. The Americans were outnumbered, and the British had the local Indians on their side. Sixty of the American soldiers were killed in the attack; the rest retreated or were captured. During a lull in the battle, the other soldiers buried the dead where they fell so their bodies wouldn't be looted or scalped. It wasn't until 1815 when the war ended and the British were defeated that control of the fort was given back to the United States.

Becky stood solemnly, quietly, looking over the battlefield. The battlefield now was also the home of the Wawashkamo Golf Course. "I can't believe they put a golf course here.

"What do you mean? Seems like a good idea to me. Keeping the area mowed and nicely landscaped seems appropriate to me."

Becky looked at him, fought to control her indignation, and seemed to do so before replying. "Yes, mow it, keep it up, I'm all for that. But otherwise, leave it alone. You don't put a damned golf course here. Sixty American soldiers died fighting for their country here. They were buried where they fell. So how do we honor their sacrifice? We walk all over their graves playing golf! Why not just put a golf course over Gettysburg, or Arlington? It's the same damned thing. This is a total outrage."

Tim swallowed and took a few steps back from Becky, feeling uneasy. She noticed this reaction and suddenly grinned. She took a deep breath and looked around.

"It's okay. I'm fine. I'm very unhappy the way these veterans are being treated though. To me it's criminal. I can feel the outrage the soldiers feel about the way their sacrifices are being honored." Becky seemed to calm, her anger subsiding rapidly.

"But I also know this course will never be closed. So we might as well ride on. But that's not going to stop me from sending a letter to the Governor letting her know my outrage." Tim seemed to relax. He nodded briefly, and they rode on.

Twenty minutes later they ended up on the eight-mile perimeter road that circled the outside of the island. From this point it would be four miles back to town. They'd be able to see the water again, and actually know they were on an island.

The halfway point was also called the British Landing. This was where in 1812, British troops landed secretly then made their way inland to surround Fort Mackinac. Badly outnumbered and taken by complete surprise, the Americans surrendered without firing a shot. They hadn't received the notice that Britain had declared war and the War of 1812 had begun.

"So the battlefield in the center of the island, that was when the Americans tried to get the fort back, but lost?" asked Tim.

Becky nodded. "Yes, but we lost that battle too. It wasn't until the U.S. won the war that we got control of the fort again. And now I'm ready to speak to you about some of my own battles."

"If you are ready to talk about it sure, I'd like to know. *If* you're really ready to speak of it now."

Becky smiled. "Yes, I'm ready. Come on. Let's go sit near those trees, by the water."

Once they were seated, side by side, Becky said, "Okay, here is the deal…" She told the story about what happened in El Salvador, how Billy had left her and Jack alone with an injured soldier, outnumbered and under attack from radical guerillas, how Jack had been killed and how unapologetic Billy had been about it all. She further explained how the beat-down she had given Billy as a parting gift was far less than he deserved. After she was done she looked at Tim, trying to gauge his reaction. He looked solemn, staring at his feet.

He looked up at her finally, and in a quiet voice spoke to her. "I can understand your anger toward Billy. He was a complete coward. Geeze that must have been hard…"

"What made it harder was being in love with Billy, or at least thinking I was, and having him betray us all like that. And Jack. …I failed him," she said softly. Tim put a hand on her back and rubbed.

"I'm very sorry. I mean that. I'm very sorry. I guess I don't know what to say. But it wasn't your fault. You and Ashley did all you could. It was Billy's fault, not yours. It's no wonder you reacted like you did. If I could find him right now I would kick his ass, too!"

"Oh, we won't have to find him. He will find us. He and his newfound rich buddies will stop at nothing to find those gold coins. But I'll be damned if I'm gonna let Billy find it. I think I'll take you up on your earlier offer. Do you still want to do some diving around the wreck of the *Voyager* tomorrow?"

"I would love to help you keep that gold out of the hands of that traitor and his obnoxious cronies. Count me in. Now, let's get back to town, I'm hungry," said Tim.

About thirty minutes later they rode into a very busy town. The tourists had arrived for the day and were everywhere. They were in the process of looking for a place to eat when they ran into Sara, who greeted them warmly. She told them the story of the missing diver and the one who'd gotten the bends.

"Do you think they were looking for the gold? asked Tim.

"Most likely. There has been nothing found of the second diver, nothing at all. The boat's intact, no problem at all. Looks like another, well you know…" Sara's voice trailed off.

"We were going to look tomorrow, I mean, go diving. What do you think?" asked Tim, feeling a sudden chill.

Sara shrugged. "I wish I knew. I can't ignore all these disappearances, but as a scientist, I can't really believe in triangles and curses and such."

"That photo we saw from the buoy looked like a ghost, a specter to me. And here's something else to consider, what made the other person surface so quickly? Something must have scared him to risk the bends like that," said Becky.

Sara nodded in agreement. "That's for sure. Perhaps he saw that ghost or spirit or whatever it was in the photos. It seems like when people are looking for the gold is when they disappear. I mentioned this to Archie and he flipped out, I mean totally flipped out. He didn't want to hear anything about my theory. But the fact is people disappear when they are near the possible location of the gold or are looking for it."

"But so many different places? People and boats are vanishing lots of places in the area," said Tim.

"Perhaps the ghost or curse or whatever it is we saw in those pictures keeps moving it around, after he makes the people and boats vanish. Just to try to keep his gold safer," suggested Sara.

"You really think it's the evil spirit of Teller cursing it?" asked Becky quietly.

Sara threw up her hands. "Who knows? I really don't believe in curses, at least I don't want to. But something is going on. And we humans don't understand or know everything. Even though we like to think we do."

"Maybe we should forget about our dive," suggested Tim.

"Just be very alert and cautious. I don't want you guys becoming a statistic." She glanced at her watch. "Hey, look, I better get back to the lab. Lamas will freak if I'm gone much longer!" Waving, Sara hurried off to the lab.

"Still want to dive tomorrow?" asked Tim.

Becky nodded. "If you still want to, you bet."

Tim grinned. "Hell yes! Besides, I feel really safe with a tough chick like you watching my back." He stepped forward and hugged her. She pulled back, obviously surprised, looking uncomfortable with what had just happened.

Tim immediately felt guilty. "Sorry, something came over me. I just had to hug you."

Becky gave him a thin smile. "It's okay. I just wasn't expected it that's all. Come on, let's eat. I swear I can smell those caramelized onions for those pot roast sandwiches over at the Yankee Rebel Tavern."

Tim chuckled. "Pot roast sandwiches it is. I wonder if I can get provolone instead of cheddar?"

Becky joined in his laughter and they headed toward Astor Street.

* * *

Billy, Ellison and Steele watched from a discreet distance.

"Most likely talking about that diver that disappeared," mused Billy.

"Yeah, but what about the other one? The one that surfaced so quickly he got the bends? We all know *why* he surfaced so quickly. He saw the same thing we saw," said Ellison. Worried wrinkles crisscrossed his face.

"Let them have the treasure. Come on, let's find another treasure to look for somewhere else," begged Ellison. Steele shook his head firmly.

"No way will I give up twenty million that we are so close to getting. Besides, we don't have to do the looking anyway, do we Billy?"

"No, I'm sure that scientist lady told them where those guys were diving. And knowing Becky like I do, she'll want to go and look for the gold. She loves adventure and excitement. And the fact is since one of those guys disappeared and the other was apparently swimming away from this whatever-it-is you saw shows they were very close to the gold. So, we just tail them," said Billy.

Ellison's face brightened. "So they dive for the gold, hopefully find it, and when they surface with the chest we just take it."

"Exactly. They do all the diving, face all the danger, and *we* get all the rewards. Nothing could easier. Billy, you keep them in sight. Carl and I are going shopping for some rifles in Mackinaw City. We'll go to the big sporting goods store in the Mackinaw Crossings. I forgot the name of it."

"Rifles?" Billy was suddenly uneasy.

"Yes of course. You don't think they will just hand that chest over to us do you? We'll need to have a display of force to get it from them."

"Just a display, nobody gets hurt, right?" insisted Billy.

"That's up to your friends, and how much they cooperate," replied Steele bluntly.

"But we will do whatever necessary to get that gold. The two of us didn't get to our current positions being passive," put in Carl for good measure.

Billy watched them go, wondering what he'd got himself into.

* * *

After eating, Becky and Tim headed up to Fort Mackinac, on a high bluff overlooking the downtown and surrounding waters. It was built in 1715, and served as an active fort as recently as 1936, when it was finally closed and added to the state park commission list of tourist attractions. It was kept up meticulously, and was in excellent condition. Costumed persons worked the various areas of the fort while manikins in other areas completed the scene.

They walked around to the various buildings of the fort, marveling at the original equipment used in those days, and the toughness these people exhibited in their lives, doing almost everything by hand and having very little technology to help them.

"We sure are soft compared to the way these people were. I mean, even the families lived here, not just the soldiers. The women, the children, they all had to be so strong just to survive," said Tim genuinely impressed.

Becky nodded her head in agreement. "They were a rare breed, that's for sure."

As they left the building that had served as the fort headquarters, Tim prodded Becky and pointed to elderly women standing in the grassy open area in the center of the fort that had served as the parade field. They had their hands in the air like they were praying, yet they seemed to be talking to themselves. They turned in slow circles, hands still raised, still talking.

Becky motioned Tim to follow her and they approached the two ladies.

"What's up?" asked Becky as she approached. One of the women cast an annoyed look at Becky, but lowered her hands. She exhaled slowly, and her companion did the same.

"We are from the Southern Michigan Psychic Society. We speak to those that have preceded us. And you have interrupted us speaking to the dead soldiers and family members who once lived here."

Tim nodded and said, "So what did they tell you if I might be so bold to ask?"

The other lady looked at Tim with disapproval on her face. "You are a non-believer. Why should we tell you?"

Tim shrugged. "I didn't say I didn't believe. I know that some people most likely do have psychic ability. It is those who have figured out or have the ability to use that amount of their brainpower. But hey, if you can't tell us what the soldiers once here told you, that's fine," declared Tim.

Becky suppressed a smile.

"Very well, non-believer. I shall tell you, so that you may come to greater knowledge of the spiritual world. There is great sadness here. It was a harsh life. Men dying in battle, families left fatherless. Despair, much despair."

"What do you think, Becky?" asked Tim. Becky looked around the fort, her face taking on that blank stare again. She nodded her head a few times, and again exhaled.

"You two are sadly mistaken," she announced. The women's faces turned deep crimson. Lines of anger crisscrossed their faces.

"How dare you! We know."

Becky cut them off. "Look, if you don't actually feel the soldiers here, then don't make up lies. There is no sadness here. The people here liked being stationed here. They enjoyed it. For the most part it was a happy place. You defile their memory with your dammed circus act."

The two women seemed shocked beyond belief, and were unable to speak. Finally they settled for sauntering off.

Becky and Tim quickly forgot about the incident, and enjoyed seeing the rest of the fort. They watched a demonstration of firing one of the fort's cannons, and of the rifles used during the era.

By the end of the day they were both thoroughly exhausted. They were quiet on the ferry ride back to Mackinaw City; in fact they nearly fell asleep. As they arrived at their apartment complex, Tim was tired, but in a pleasant, satisfied way. He was infused with warm, loving feelings toward Becky. He had thoroughly enjoyed his time with her, and felt they had grown much closer over the past hours. Every nerve in his body was suddenly alert and attuned to her presence at his side. He turned to her and smiled, then finally letting himself do what he'd wanted to do all day, he took Becky in his arms and kissed her long and deep. Then he stood back, ready to feel her wrath.

Becky was initially shocked at the sudden passion he showed, so much so she wasn't sure how to react. So she did the only thing she figured she could, she let him continue. But Becky wasn't quite ready to let her guard down just yet. So when Tim leaned forward to kiss her yet again, Becky stopped him.

"You best get some sleep, in your own apartment. I'll be over at eight sharp. Then we'll get some gear and do some treasure hunting," said Becky.

Tim nodded. He smiled as though she'd given him a present and said, "Okay, got it, goodnight."

Unwilling to juggle her mixed emotions in his presence, Becky hurried to her door, quickly turned the key, entered and nearly slammed the door behind her. Leaning her back against the wooden surface, she sighed. She was doing it again. She was falling for a man. Damn! She didn't want that to happen again, not with any man. Her inner voice told her she could trust Tim in a way it had never told her she could trust Billy. Or had it? Was her voice really telling her that? Or was that just what she wanted it to tell her?

Becky walked through the bedroom to her balcony and looked out over the darkening straits. She could see the lights of businesses lining the main street of Mackinac Island. Her thoughts changed, and she wondered about the disappearances. All that water out there. The Great Lakes were basically fresh-water oceans. In fact the early explorers thought they had indeed discovered small fresh-water oceans. What could be causing these people and ships to vanish? Was there a curse? If they dove for the gold tomorrow would they too become statistics? Becky shook her head and laughed lightly. *Just dive, pay attention, and use proper dive techniques and you'll be fine,* she counseled herself. She permitted herself another smile and returned to her room, determined to get a good night's sleep.

Billy watched the scene from a safe distance with mixed emotions. He was still angry at the way Becky had roughed him up in El Salvador, and he still wanted to rectify that. On the other hand, he still cared for her very much, and was hoping there was a chance to win her back. She just needed to be tamed by a real man. Though she had kissed this Tim whoever he was, she'd refused him another kiss. Perhaps that could mean an opening for him yet. And with his newfound friends, they could make sure they got the gold even if Becky found it first.

He would have to take it of course, and his friends could just buy Tim off so he'd walk out on Becky. Billy figured all he had to say was the reason they took the gold was to expose Tim for what a fraud he really was. Then Becky would agree to come back to him, and they could have the future he knew was meant to be. Billy smiled to himself. It was a perfect plan.

For his part, Tim just wanted to sleep tonight. It had been a long and busy day and the bed felt awfully good to him as he flopped down. He smiled thinking of the kiss. After the way Billy had stabbed her in the back, that had to have been quite a step for Becky. Tim hoped that if he just went slowly now, he had a real chance to develop something with her--if only he could continue to work past his lack of self-confidence.

He tried not to worry about it overmuch. That just made him feel stressed out, which added pressure to any potentially dangerous situations. When things got tense he panicked and reacted badly. Why? Why would he do that? He had to solve that problem, and quickly if he had any hope at all of a relationship with Becky. She'd already been burned by a man running out on her, and she would never tolerate a man too weak to stand toe-to-toe with her in a tough situation.

Tim didn't really understand why he had this problem. He just wasn't very good when it came to a confrontation. The only thing he could reason was that he'd tried his entire life to win his dad's approval. It was his dad who told him going to the academy would make a man out if him. He'd always thought he would be good at it, thus making a good state policeman. That way he could help people too. So why when people really needed to count on him did he cave?

The look on his dad's face when he had to confess that he'd failed his final flashed before his eyes. It was the same look he imagined would be on Becky's face if he ever let her down when she was depending on him. He realized he couldn't let that happen if he wanted any future with Becky. He could see the time coming when she would have to confront Ellison, Steele and Billy. And when that time occurred, he knew Becky would need him by her side as an active partner, not a frozen zombie. He had to act like a real man if he wanted any chance of a future with Becky at all.

Tim sighed. He knew what he had to do.

Chapter 7

Becky woke up and looked around her apartment. The smile widened on her lips. No dreams. No reliving the incident in El Salvador.

She wasn't worried about Billy and his newfound rich buddies. She'd noticed Billy following them, most likely as a spy for Steele and Ellison. It was obvious they intended to tail them and take the gold should they find it. They might even get violent in order to take it from them. But what if they decided to pull guns? Becky figured she had two choices then. She could get a concealed weapons permit and carry it with her, or she could do nothing. Becky knew in a regular fight she could probably take all three of them at once, especially if Tim helped her.

But would Tim be able to overcome his critical flaw and help her? He seemed very intimidated by them on the island. They nearly backed him down, and that bothered her. She wondered if he'd had an overbearing father who out of respect and upbringing he'd obeyed without question. It would explain why he hesitated to overrule a perp when confronted with an authority figure.

He was well aware of his shortcomings and seem to be working hard to overcome them, like he was disgusted with himself for his mistakes. Becky was going to remain on her guard. She wasn't about to give another man her trust, and then find herself being burned by that man. As much as she liked him, Tim was on a very short leash with her.

Becky left the apartment, went to Tim's and when he didn't respond banged until she finally got him to open the door.

He was sleepy-eyed and drowsy, obviously having been awakened by her knock. He motioned for her to come in and pointed toward the coffee maker, whose timer apparently worked better than his alarm clock.

"I'll just be a second getting ready."

Becky helped herself to a cup as he disappeared into his bathroom. The shower turned on, and ten minutes later, just after she finished watching the weather report on TV, he reappeared awakened and ready to go.

"Sorry about that," he said, eagerly accepting the mug she held out to him, chuckling. "Had some trouble sleeping last night. Too much excitement ahead for today."

"No problem. Let's get going though. First we'll go get all the gear we need at the Mackinaw City dive shop. They can give us a listing of boat rentals. I figured we can just rent a pontoon. They're stable, easy to maneuver and perfect for diving," said Becky.

The twosome picked up all their necessary dive gear, and were pointed toward a good boat rental just a few blocks down the road.

As they secured the pontoon rental, the owner glanced at their dive gear and was suddenly less than anxious to rent.

"You two are scuba diving? Let me guess, to the *Voyager* wreck?" Becky nodded.

"Look, lots of people and boats vanish looking for the gold, I don't want to lose this boat."

"We are just diving on the wreck, not looking for gold. If the gold was right by the wreck, it would have been found years ago," Tim pointed out. Becky smiled a little to herself. Of course, they were going to swim away from the wreck a bit just to see what else might be out there, just in case.

The man still looked uneasy, but finally nodded his head slowly.

"Okay, but I'm going to want a larger deposit, just in case my boat never returns. This is business after all."

"No problem, but isn't that what insurance is for?"

"That all takes time, raises my premium, and in the meantime I lose out on rental fees."

"Look, can we hitch it up now?" asked Becky, sighing her impatience.

"Yeah, go ahead," grumbled the man.

After about five minutes the boat was loaded with their gear, and they were ready to head out. Becky took the pilot's wheel and headed the boat toward the wreck of the *Voyager*.

As they cruised along, they passed other private boats, and were in turn passed by a couple of ferryboats taking excited tourists to Mackinac Island. Tim studied the water chart.

"You know the wreck is marked with a white buoy. I can see it in fact, just about fifty yards farther up."

Tim squinted, straining to see ahead. He could indeed make out the white blob getting larger and larger. Becky stopped about twenty feet from the buoy and dropped anchor.

"Okay, let's get our gear on and have some fun!" she said excitedly. They helped each other into their dive gear, and checked and double-checked all the equipment. They also reviewed hand signals to make they were on the same page.

"And if we see something that shouldn't be there, don't just swim fast to the surface, you don't want to end up like that other diver," instructed Becky.

Tim felt heat prickle around his neck. He looked uneasy. "What if something is down there?"

"We stay alert and be prepared," responded Becky quickly, with authority.

"Okay, okay, I get it," responded Tim.

A few moments later they plunged into the cold waters of Lake Huron. As they did so a ferryboat sped by full of tourists. The wake hit them, pushing both of them a few feet from where they had intended to start the dive. Shaking her head, Becky motioned for Tim to follow her. She swam on top of the water to the buoy marking the wreck. Then she let air out of her vest and began the descent.

* * *

Three sets of binoculars trained on the twosome from a discreet distance. Steele lowered his as they sunk below the waves.

"They pretend to be looking at the wreck, but they are looking for the gold too no doubt," he stated with certainty. Ellison shrugged it off.

"They don't seem to be in the right place though. That isn't really where we found the chest."

"True, but it could be in a different place now, you know what I mean," replied Steele. Ellison's eyes grew a little wider at the memory, as he nodded his head.

"What do you guys mean by that?" asked Billy.

"It means that thing we saw that ruined our sub could have moved the gold to a different place, to keep it safe. It makes perfect sense. That's why the gold hasn't ever been found, except for a few coins here and there. Because the curse, the ghost, the spirit or whatever it is keeps moving it around after people locate it," said Steele.

"After it makes them and their boats a statistic of course," added Ellison for good measure.

"I wonder where they disappear to," mumbled Billy in fear.

"We don't intend to find out. That's why we let your girlfriend and her new guy do all the work, and we take the gold from them. That is assuming they actually find the gold and are able to return to the boat with the gold without vanishing first," said Steele. Though he didn't like the current conversation, Billy could only nod his head in agreement. This was a one in a lifetime chance for him to get ahead in life. He wasn't about to let anything or anybody, including Becky, get in his way.

There was no doubt how ruthless these two people were, but Billy needed them and their resources. And once they did take the gold from them should they find it, he was certain he could convince Becky of the rightfulness of their actions. They'd had something special at one point, not even she would deny that. Billy was sure he could get the two of them back to the way they once were, and then the twosome could have a fairytale life together.

* * *

A rope attached to the buoy went all the way down to where the *Voyager* lay in twenty-five feet of water. Holding on to the rope, Becky and Tim slowly pulled themselves down to the wreck. About every five feet they stopped, pinched their noses and blew, thus clearing their ears and allowing them to descend safely to greater depths.

At twenty-three feet they got the first glimpse of the wreck. It seemed to be in excellent condition. The cold, fresh water of the Great Lakes preserved shipwrecks very well. They swam over to it, getting their first close up look. Becky pulled up the camera attached by a line to her wrist and began to snap photos. The *Voyager* was on the side of a downward grade, so the ship was tilted slightly to the left. They had about twenty feet of visibility, so they had an excellent view.

They began swimming along the side of the ship, Tim running his hands across the wooden planks, while Becky kept snapping photos. Becky wondered what had gone through the mind of those military people that had been on the ship. What had they thought when the call came out that they were being attacked by Indians and pirates? And what had caused Teller to become a traitor? Did he not even care that many of his comrades would be killed in the attack?

Becky shook her head. Of course he hadn't cared. Otherwise he would never have plotted this whole thing. She felt anger flush her cheeks in the cold water. It was a good thing she hadn't been alive then. It would have been a pleasure for her to personally take care of Teller.

Becky snapped herself back to the present and began to look over the ship some more. She was amazed at the condition it had been preserved in. The cold water kept the wooden planks in almost mint condition. Becky mused that someone could almost raise the ship, repair it and use it yet again. It would be great to see the ship on land as a museum. It would be an excellent addition to the fort either in Mackinaw City or on the island. But it was also a good idea to let the ship lie in the water. It served as a fitting memorial to the men who had served and died on her.

Becky looked around and saw Tim had passed the length of the ship, and was now swimming in open waters. He seemed to be looking at something. He turned, and motioned for Becky to follow. Becky sped forward, catching up to Tim, and saw for the first time what he was looking at. She caught her breath. It appeared to be a chest, about thirty feet away.

Becky frowned into the mouthpiece. This didn't make sense. If the chest was so easy to find, why hadn't it been found before? Her eyes grew wide as an idea began to formulate in her mind. She discarded it, but it popped back in. Of course it made perfect sense.

Becky was suddenly alert. Her senses were talking to her. No, they were shouting at her. She saw Tim swimming just ahead of her. He was fine, just approaching the chest. She sucked in extra air and took a slow look behind. Yes, there it was. It was the same bluish-gray form they had seen in the photographs from the buoy. It appeared like it was already reaching arm-like extensions toward her.

Becky dashed forward, grabbing Tim's leg. In confusion he looked at her with a *"what's wrong?"* look on his face. She pointed emphatically at the blue cloud rapidly approaching. Tim's eyes grew wide in terror. He quickly abandoned his inspection of the chest and began to kick furiously to the surface. Becky again restrained him, motioning for him to slow down. Getting the bends wouldn't solve anything. Tim resisted her efforts at first, but slowed after Becky grabbed him by the throat and squeezed ever so slightly, her eyes showing she was in no mood to fight with him.

Tim nodded, and slowed his ascent, while Becky motioned for him to continue. Becky spun and swam away from Tim, taking the ghostly figure with her. As Becky arrived at the chest, she noticed some of the coins had fallen out, from a small opening in the chest that had seemed to have rotted away. She grabbed a handful of the coins and placed them into the collection bag at her waist. She glanced at Tim. He was nearly out of her view now. Good. That meant he was almost to the surface. Now she just had to figure a way to get away from this whatever it was.

Becky pulled out her dive knife, thought about it, and put it away. She doubted the knife would be much good against whatever this thing was. She began to slowly surface, taking another handful of gold coins with her. The thing got within twenty feet of her, its ghostly arms again stretching out to her. At that moment Becky took the coins in her hand and tossed them away, watching them glitter as they tumbled to the sandy bottom. The form seemed to hesitate slightly, then followed the coins as they floated to the bottom. Becky quickly snapped off several photos of the blue cloud with the waterproof camera corded to her dive belt and then increased her ascent as quickly as she dared, finally hitting the surface.

She glanced around, half expecting to see the form surface and attack her once more, but the attack never came. Instead she saw Tim pulling up next to her in the boat. Becky got her flippers off and climbed the ladder into the pontoon.

"We have company," said Tim, motioning to the west. A large private yacht approached, pulling alongside of them. There was little doubt who was in the boat.

"Just play it cool. I will handle this," said Becky firmly, her tone suggesting she was in no mood to compromise. Tim nodded, still smarting at the way he'd lost his cool in the water. It dawned on him that incident could have ruined his chances with Becky for good.

"Helloooo..!" Billy shouted from the lavish yacht.

"You don't have to shout. You're just next to us. I can hear you fine," said Becky.

"How did your dive go?" asked Steele, appearing on deck with Ellison and Billy.

"Just fine. It was a lot of fun," said Becky.

"We got some good pics of the *Voyager* wreck," put in Tim.

"You didn't happen to find the chest did you?" asked Ellison.

"You see a chest anywhere?" mocked Becky.

"My new friends and I really want that chest, so if you should happen to find it, you'd be wise to turn it over to us. We need the funding to continue our downstate business ventures," remarked Billy, an almost evil grin appearing on his lips.

"Don't have a big enough yacht, is that it?" asked Becky, her tone still mocking them.

"Billy is our new partner, so we need extra funding for him," explained Ellison.

"Be good chaps and turn over that chest to us should you find it," said Steele. As he spoke the last words he pulled out a twenty-gauge shotgun and laid it over his shoulder.

"Ya'll have a nice day now," finished Steele. He nodded to Billy who took control of the yacht. It made a slow arc away from the pontoon boat.

"So where to now?" asked Tim.

"Home, but tomorrow at work we need a long talk with Sara and Lamas. They need to know that *thing* is out there. I got some pretty good photos of it while I was holding it off you.

When they arrived back at Tim's apartment, Becky finally expressed her displeasure with Tim. She bluntly pointed out the fact that, "I need to know now where you're coming from. I already know about the academy, but are you going to be able to move past it? Your initial reaction today was panic, and you let Billy and his new buddies nearly back you down when we first met them on the island. I want to know what the deal is, *now.*"

Tim could only sigh. He nodded. "It's like when the pressure's on, I just sort of lose it. I get flustered and fall apart, making bad decisions. When things are calm or I'm just taking a written test, I'm fine. I guess I just don't perform well under pressure. Until I took that final exam, even I didn't know that about myself. I did fine in the practice scenarios, but fell apart during the final. It was like everything I learned in the lectures and books I suddenly forgot. I'm sorry Becky, I really am."

Becky sat back and looked at Tim, thinking deeply. They had become friends. She wasn't going to deny that much, at least. Somehow, he needed to overcome his problem. She wondered if there was anything she could do to help.

"I'm glad you told me the truth, I really am. I appreciate your honesty. But as things continue on, I need you to try and overcome your tendency to crack under pressure, because things could get even worse," Becky said.

"What do you mean?" asked Tim. Becky pulled out her dive pouch and poured out some of the gold coins. Tim's mouth gaped as he looked over the coins.

"According to history, Teller said he'd go after anyone near his gold. So it is just possible, his ghost or spirit or whatever it was we saw under the water could be looking for us even up here. That is assuming he can actually do those things that he stated before he was executed."

Tim felt his neck suddenly get warm, and he rubbed at it to still the fine hairs that had raised.

"What do you think, can he really do those things?"

Becky shrugged. "Well, something is causing the disappearances of the boats and people. Is it something to do with Teller and the curse? Maybe, maybe not. Maybe it's just bad boat piloting by people. But you yourself admitted to seeing something down there."

Tim reached out and examined one of the coins. He wondered if they really could cause the ghost to come after them. Though he knew it was okay to be afraid, even normal, he needed to become braver, to learn to do the right thing in a wrong situation, despite his fear.

* * *

The bluish ghost-haze surveyed the coins that had fallen from the chest, and coaxed them back inside. He was very annoyed. The waves on the surface of the water suddenly tripled in size as his annoyance became even greater. He was losing more and more gold, and that was simply not acceptable. The haze enveloped the chest and moved it to yet another location, this time again attaching it to a nearby buoy. The haze turned a shade of crimson when it realized suddenly that even more of the coins were missing than it had originally thought. Now it was time to go above the water to dry land to find out where this female had taken his coins.

Chapter 8

The next day, Becky and Tim turned over the coins to Archie Lamas and Sara. Sara was flabbergasted at the story, but Lamas wasn't moved. As usual he brushed it off, saying they were seeing things under the water, easily frightened because of all the wild tales.

Sara quickly developed the photos Becky had taken, which clearly showed the bluish form. She thrust them at Lamas, a hint of anger in her tone. "Did they hallucinate these?" she demanded.

He stared at the photos a long time. "Okay, I admit this looks like a person."

"Not just a person." Sara pulled out two old photos that were of Lieutenant Teller. The photos Becky took were close enough to actually reveal facial features in the bluish mist. There was a definite resemblance, though it was somewhat vague.

"So you're saying this mist is actually Teller's ghost who has come forward in time to protect what he always considered to be his gold?" asked Lamas.

"Yes," answered Sarah quickly.

"And he is responsible for the disappearances of boats and people in the area?"

"Most certainly. When people come too close he takes action, making them disappear. And don't ask me where to. I don't know. Most likely we will never find out. Where do ghosts live when they aren't haunting someplace? Who knows for sure?" said Sara.

"I can't believe I'm standing here and actually listening to all this," said Lamas suddenly. "This has to be a crock."

"Put it this way," interjected Becky quietly, but just loud enough to get the others' attention. "We don't know everything, we just think we do. Things like being physic or ESP, wormholes, time wraps, that sort of thing. Much is out there we don't understand. So we should never shut our minds down entirely."

Lamas sighed, and nodded his head slowly. "Okay, let's say you're right about all this. In ten days we have the Fourth of July, and this year it's on a Friday, which means for many people, it's a three-day weekend. Independence Day is always very busy up here, but this year it will be busier than usual. We've got about fifty thousand people about to descend on us, and at least a few thousand will be bringing boats and yachts up. The Straits will be full of boats. We will also have at least a few hundred of these people scuba diving. The Coast Guard will have its hands full taking care of accidents and drunks on the water. How in hell do we protect all those people and stop Teller from making them vanish to wherever the hell they vanish to?"

"I don't know that we can. Our only hope is that no boaters or divers come too close to wherever the gold is," put in Tim.

"What can't we do?" The group looked up to see Steve Grant arrive with Coast Guard Commander Oslo.

"We had another boat with four people onboard vanish last night. They said something seemed to be after them, and that they were near some buoy. Then, poof, nothing but static. We've scoured the straits three times, nothing. So I assume you have some news for me that might shed some light on what may have happened to this and many other boats and people in the area.

Lamas nodded slowly. "Yes we do…but you're not going to believe it. I'm not sure I believe it."

"Right now, I'm open to anything," replied Commander Oslo.

"Okay, here goes." Lamas then relayed the story and photos provided by Becky and Tim. The commander looked sharply at Becky, and studied the photos carefully. He looked over the coins.

"Airman Vasquez, this is all right? I have your word as a military member you didn't fake any of this?" asked the commander.

"Yes sir, you do. None of this was faked. Tim Green here was there with me," answered Becky in a serious tone. The commander nodded, and looked over at Tim.

"You confirm this story?"

Tim nodded firmly. "Yes, I do. You can put me on a polygraph if you want," responded Tim.

"That won't be necessary. Okay then. I would suggest two things should happen. I could get these coins appraised. I would presume you'd like to know how rich you are now?"

Becky grinned. "I admit, I am rather curious about that."

"What else do you recommend, sir?" asked Tim.

"Airman, I will give you a receipt for the coins, and I suggest they be put in a secure safe at the St. Ignace Coast Guard Station immediately."

Becky seemed confused by the sudden look of concern on the commander's face. "Why?" asked Becky.

"Think about the story of these coins, what Teller said in his final words before the execution was carried out. He said that he would haunt the coins. That means if someone somehow gets the coins and chest his ghost, spirit, or whatever will be looking for that person. That means you. You don't have all of them, but I think you got enough of the coins to get his attention. You could be in danger of becoming a statistic. Let me put them in the safe at our station," finished Commander Oslo.

"We don't need monsters from the water coming ashore here, do it for our safety!" exclaimed Steve Grant.

Tim suppressed a smile. His boss still worried about monsters, and he might actually be on to something for once.

"So you believe in the curse then?" asked Becky.

The commander shrugged. "These photos are mighty convincing. And I have no explanation for the disappearances in the area. So for now, yeah, I'm going to believe, at least off the record anyway. On the record I'll continue to talk to the media about boater error and excessive drinking."

"Very well then, commander, take the coins, but I'll keep just one of them, just to have." replied Becky.

"Which gets us back to the original topic. How do we protect the hundreds or thousands of boaters and divers that will be arriving in the next seven to ten days?" asked Lamas, seemingly annoyed by the change in topic.

"I'll have two cutters out there, keeping an eye on things. We've also contracted some civilian security agencies; they will have eight more boats constantly cruising the straits. That's about all I can do," replied Commander Oslo.

"We'll try to downplay everything about the triangle and curse at the tours in the lab. The last thing we want to do is scare away tourists," commented Lamas.

* * *

The bluish haze seeped out of Lake Huron like a fog gently rolling onto the land from the sea. It changed once it was fully on land, from being thirty feet long to six feet tall. It now looked like a typical tourist, blending in perfectly with the thousands of other mortals currently on the island. Now it was ready to find the rest of the coins. It was certain it wouldn't take long.

* * *

Tim left the conference room and unlocked the main doors of the research lab. The coast guard personnel had the coins in a small locked chest and walked them out of the lab, getting curious looks from persons waiting to take the first tour of the lab. Billy, Steele and Ellison were standing outside, away from the other tourists. They tried to get closer to the coast guard persons with the chest, but were promptly pushed away. They turned their attention to Becky and Tim next.

"You must have found something good under the water huh?" asked Steele. Tim felt nervous, then became angry. What business was it of Billy's?

Becky noticed Tim's agitation and decided to handle the conversation herself. "What makes you think so?"

"I wouldn't think the coast guard would be involved if you hadn't," put in Billy.

"You should be careful, very careful. If word got around that you may have found some of the lost coins, well…so many people own guns these days. It could turn deadly," said Ellison in a sinister tone, an evil smile slowly expanding on his lips.

Becky and Tim didn't need to be hit over the head to get the hidden message.

"Thanks for the warning," said Becky coolly.

Tim was no longer able to keep still. "Yeah, thanks. That was real neighborly of you three. And you," he said with mounting anger directed at Billy, "have a lot of nerve even showing your face around Becky after you ran away like a frightened little girl and left her and the rest of your team alone in the jungle with a gang of rebel gorillas. Do you really believe she'd ever consider doing more than kick your ass again?"

Billy's face turned beet red. He started forward, but Steel reached out to grab his shoulder. "Not now," he said, glancing around at all the tourists.

"Another time," said Steele.

"You can count on it," Tim responded.

The three men turned and walked away, quickly, apparently wanting to avoid any public association with anyone who might become a future victim of their greed.

"Let it go, Superman."

Tim turned to look at Becky, grinning proudly. He hadn't even had to force himself to stand up to Billy and the other bastards. He had been so offended for Becky, and so disgusted at the jerk's arrogant attitude, he had seriously wanted to punch him in the mouth and close it permanently.

Becky chuckled and said, "I think you may be getting over your little problem, Tim. I'm really proud of you for standing up to Billy and those dressed up thugs.

"I know you didn't need me to stand up for you, but I am seriously sick of that tool."

"I don't blame you," Becky said. "I understand better than anyone how angry Billy can make you. Come on, let's get to work. We've wasted enough time on that traitor."

* * *

The specter's human form decided to call himself Tom, and watched closely as the two walked back into the building. These were the people under water that took his coins. But the question was, did they still have them? It seemed like the other military people might have taken them somewhere. Tom would have to join the tour. That way he could get close enough to the female to read her thoughts.

* * *

The group entered the lab and Becky gathered them around.

"First, for security reasons we have to check all of you for anything that might be a threat to this facility. Sorry, a sign of the times, even in the obscure north." As she finished, Tim began doing his checks. He noticed one person seemed to look somewhat pale.

"Are you okay, sir?" The man gave a small smile. He indeed looked pale, his eyes a very pale blue, almost whitish in appearance. Tim felt suddenly ill at ease around the man.

"I am fine. My name is Tom. Why do you ask?"

Tim tried to hide his uneasiness. "You look a little pale is all."

"I'm fine. I had a bout with the flu a few days ago. I may not have completely regained my strength." The man's voice seemed to slither out of his mouth like a snake. For whatever reason, Tim just wanted to get as far away from this man as possible.

Becky approached the twosome with a puzzled look on her face.

"Everything okay here?"

Tom smiled. "Of course, your co-worker noticed I seem somewhat pale. I guess my recent illness still hasn't completely gone away. Becky looked at the man and her eyes narrowed. Her inner voice was speaking to her, giving her a warning that this wasn't a good man. Becky did her best to pretend she was concerned. "Are you well enough to stay on the tour?" asked Becky.

"I wouldn't miss it," replied the man.

Becky lipped her sweetest smile. "Very well, then continue we shall."

She turned away and frowned. Something was wrong about that man. He was different somehow, and not in a good way. Becky did her best to continue the tour as if nothing was wrong.

The man asked several questions about the voyager wreck, and the lost gold. He was especially interested to know how many of the coins may have been recovered or if she knew who had recovered them. Becky put an end to his interrogation by saying she had no idea who or if anyone had ever recovered any of the coins. Becky was thankful that the man finally shut up for the rest of the tour.

"Thank you for your informative tour. I must leave now," the man said dismissively as she bid the tour goodbye. The rest of the tour also left, and Becky and Tim decided to follow the strange man. They nearly caught up to him when they saw him approach into Billy, Steele and Ellison. Steele approached the man quickly, while Becky and Tim edged closer to hear well.

"I understand you have been asking a lot about that lost gold out there," said Steele.

The pale man seemed surprised. "How did you find out so quickly?"

"Money talks. It's that simple. Now listen up. That gold is ours. My friend and I always get what we want. Our other friend here is a former military commando, and he's here to make sure we get what we want this time, too."

Becky snorted, hearing this last statement. What a joke. Billy actually had the balls to tell these guys he was a military commando? She tried her best to control her laughter and not give away their location around the corner.

Billy approached the man with a swagger. "Just forget about the gold and go treasure hunting somewhere else. You don't understand what you're up against."

The pale man smiled then, and it was a chilling expression that had nothing to do with humor. "No, *you* don't." He grabbed Billy by the throat and hurled him twenty feet through the air, spilling him hard on the ground. Apparently the flu hadn't effected his throwing arm. Steele and Ellison looked shocked at the sudden turn of events. They both backed up from the man, looked around for aid.

"If you three will excuse me now, I have errands to run." The man calmly walked away as if nothing had happened.

"Did you see that?" Tim asked, eyes wide and disbelieving.

"Yeah..." said Becky, immobilized with shock.

Billy had struggled to his feet in the meantime and was trying to get his bearings. Ellison and Steele hurried over to him. "Damn...who was that? *What* was that?" asked Billy.

"He looked weird as hell..." began Ellison.

"Yeah...almost like that thing we saw that wrecked the sub. The face seemed the same."

"So that means the gold, or at least part of it could be around somewhere?" asked Billy.

"Good, while this thing is looking on land, we can get ourselves another sub in the water and look again for the chest," said Steele. The other two nodded, silently agreeing.

Becky and Tim pulled their heads back and hugged the wall, listening intently to what was being said by the threesome.

"Wow...so that was the ghost or spirit or whatever of Teller? No wonder it was so strong. I thought something was different about that person," remarked Tim.

"If that is the case, he sure isn't a human being. H-he really is a ghost, and he's obviously after the coins I brought here," said Becky.

"It's a good thing the coast guard took them from you. Otherwise you could be in real danger. But no matter what Becky, I'm here for you and will do anything I need to protect you. In fact--" Tim stopped. He had an opening to state the truth about his feelings for Becky, but he wasn't sure this was the time. He also wasn't sure if Becky even wanted another relationship with a man. At least not this soon after the debacle she'd had with Tompkins. Maybe if he were sly enough about it she would let it go and forget about it. The more Tim thought about it, the more he thought it wasn't something that should be brought up, at least not yet.

"In fact what?" asked Becky with inquiring eyes.

Tim knew he had no way to back out now, so he plunged ahead. "The truth is, I love you, Becky," said Tim quickly, rushing the words out before he lost his nerve.

Becky's mouth was dry, and her throat tightened. This wasn't something she wanted, not at all. She liked Tim, and against every relationship experience she'd ever had, she was beginning to trust him. But, no man would ever hurt her again, ever. She was not going to fall for the same charade again. She just couldn't, not yet. Not after the way the last man stabbed her in the back. She had to learn from her mistakes.

Becky looked trouble, then turned away from Tim. He frowned, knowing he shouldn't have said anything, that it was too soon for Becky to hear those words. But he had said them, so the only thing he could do now was try to plead his case and hope for some understanding on her part.

"Listen Becky, I know why you don't want to trust men anymore after what happened. It was a terrible thing to go through and I honestly don't know how you have recovered so well."

Becky whirled around. "Look, I appreciate what you are trying to say, but no you don't understand. Not really. How could a civilian understand? You have no clue what it was like out there. What it was like to have a teammate, more than a teammate, a man I thought I was in love with, betray me. This wasn't some video game where you get a lot of lives. This was the real deal, one chance only. Combat either bonds people or turns them into mortal enemies, forever. And the man that I trusted to have my back left me, a young girl barely old enough to drive, to die in that jungle with the rest of our team."

Becky stopped talking and turned away from Tim, sucking in more air. She swiped at her eyes and let out her breath. A few moments later, again composed, she turned back to him. "I know you want to understand. I know you feel empathy for me, but can anyone really understand how it feels to be so violated, so betrayed? Why would I ever want to love or trust another man again? Hell, for that matter, sometimes I didn't even want to live after that. I still see Jack's wife and kids crying. I still have nightmares in which I relive the entire incident. I most likely will the rest of my life. How can you ever understand that? How can anyone?" Becky's words held years of heartache, of unimaginable pain.

There was a lump in Tim's throat. It was very dry, but he was able to formulate words, though they were barely a whisper.

"I'll tell you why. I'm not Billy. Not all men betray. Look at Jack. He had a family to think about, but he didn't run off. You trusted him and he *didn't* betray your trust. That proves some men are different. *I'm* different. You just have to give me the chance to prove it. I know in the past I've kinda backed down when things got rough. And when that thing came after us diving, I admit it, I panicked. But I've learned from those experiences. I'm learning from you what it takes to really make a stand. I won't fail you, I'll do anything necessary to fight alongside you, to keep you safe."

Becky just looked at Tim with a troubled stare. All she could think was that she wished she could believe what he was saying. *Well, he did admit he has acted like a coward in the past. That can't be easy for him to say. In fact, it took a lot of integrity and bravery. No one ever wants to admit their faults. And he was right about Jack, too.*

Becky looked at her feet and finally stared back into Tim's eyes. She was struggling with her emotions and needed time to sort them out. She wasn't about to make any kind of decision at this particular moment. If Tim really did love her as he claimed, then he would be patient and wait for her to be ready to accept his love.

"We will see how things go, okay. Let's just enjoy the Fourth of July holiday weekend. We can hang out, no problem. But as for the rest, you'll have to be patient with me. That's my offer, take it or leave it."

Tim smiled. "I'll wait, I'll be patient. You're well worth waiting for."

Chapter 9

Young Coastguard Seaman Bradley yawned. He got up from the plush office chair and looked out the window into the main base. It was just starting to get dark. The sky that had been a bright cerulean all day was now a dark navy splashed with a bright orange and red flash lining the horizon over Lakes Huron and Michigan. What a sight it was! He never got tired of looking at the sunsets here.

He looked over at the base safe and shook his head. He'd been told just an hour ago it was his job to stay in the office for the night and make sure nothing disturbed the recently added contents of the safe. It made no sense to him at all, and above all ruined his plans for the evening. Well, in three days the Fourth of July holiday weekend began, so he had something to look forward to at least.

He couldn't figure out what would be so important that it had to be guarded so closely. Things were added to the safe all the time. But he knew it wasn't he job to question his orders as long as they were legal. These obviously were. All he could do was hang out for the night and do the best he could.

Bradley paced around the room a bit more and sighed yet again. This was going to be one long night. He looked out the window yet again. Then something caught his attention. The calm waters of Lake Huron weren't calm anymore. If fact, the waves appeared to be suddenly around four or five feet. That was a sudden change. He'd never seen that quick a change in the lake conditions before. Oh well, it was up to the boaters out there to pay attention to what was going on. Hopefully they all had their weather and marine radios turned on to get instant weather and sea changes.

If the people out on the water weren't paying attention to the weather or weren't listening to the radios, then the rescue people on the base could be in store for a very eventful evening themselves. He suddenly found himself happy to be stuck in the office.

* * *

The bluish-colored fog seemed to slide easily across the surface of northern Lake Huron, toward the rapidly approaching shore, kicking up large waves in its wake. It knew where its coins were, and it intended to get them back no matter what the cost. The closer it got to the coins, the stronger the aura of the coins became. It was only a matter of minutes until the coins were back with him under the water.

The specter arrived and stopped. It was the perimeter fence of a military base. No! This wasn't good. The angry spirit looked around, saw nothing, and still hesitated. Going onto a military base made it very uneasy. But it had to get its gold back. The fog-like entity slipped easily through the protective fences. In a matter of moments, it had transformed itself into a nearly normal looking person, in a coast guard uniform.

He strolled through the base, seeing only a few other people along the way. Because of his uniform, they barely gave him a nod. His senses told him that his gold was very close now, and getting closer, closer. Yes, he'd found it! It was just ahead. The ghost figure looked around, paying close attention to the sky and horizon, and saw nothing, nothing that would be a threat to it. It would appear he could safely enter this building and get the rest of his coins back.

Bradley happened to be looking out the window and saw a Seaman approaching the headquarters building. He frowned. *Now what?* he thought.

The man entered the building without knocking, and Bradley was immediately uneasy. Something was wrong with the guy. First, nobody walked into the headquarters building without knocking unless they were the commander or someone on his executive staff. And secondly, the man didn't look right. The way he moved was off somehow, wrong. As he got closer, Bradley noticed that his skin was pale, very pale, vampire pale. His hair looked more like he'd just been electrocuted, sticking out around his head like thin scarecrow straw. It was as if the guy was a mannequin come to life. He ignored Bradley and began looking around the office.

He stepped forward and Bradley gasped. The man's eyes were unnaturally translucent. Totally unnerved, Bradley slid close to the hidden alarm by the desk and began to speak to the person.

"Is there something I can do for you?" he asked, trying to be both polite and firm. The man looked at him briefly, but said nothing. He continued past him and walked to the safe. Bradley eased his hand to the base alert button on the desk, and spoke again.

"I'm going to have to ask you to get away from the safe. And since you won't tell me your business here, I think you need to leave."

The man's head turned from the safe and fixed a glare directly into his eyes. Bradley felt like he was suddenly hypnotized. The creature began to glide over to Bradley. *His legs aren't moving. It's like he's floating,* thought Bradley. The next thing he knew he was shoved rudely against the far wall. Things seemed to spin around him. He saw flashing lights, and colored circles.

Gradually his vision came back, and Bradley struggled to his feet. He half walked and half crawled to the alarm. The man was changing now, turning from a person to a bluish mist. Bradley hit the alarm, which quickly blared loudly. The mist suddenly jerked around, and Bradley could hear it speak for the first time.

"No. I need more time! You will vanish to the other place for this."

Bradley swallowed and backed up as far as he could. The mist's arms seem to envelope him. Bradley figured it was just a matter of seconds before he became another statistic. Then incredibly, the ghostly arms withdrew, the human-like mist retreated. Bradley spared a glance out the window and could see another human-like mist approaching rapidly, and more reassuring were the security coastguardsmen running in his direction.

"You were very lucky this time," the mist said before it melted away.

Released from his hypnotic daze, Bradley hurried to the door and opened it, only to come face to face with the second human mist. The security people were still about a hundred yards away, but closing in fast.

Bradley cocked his head at this ghostly figure. It was different somehow from the other one. He felt no fear at all. In fact, this one had a rather calming effect. It passed over him, and the pain in his back from being thrown against the wall by the other spirit was abruptly gone.   Then this mist too melted away.

* * *

Archie Lamas looked over at Stephen Grant, who just shrugged hopelessly.

"You're head of security for the lab. You are supposed to protect it!" thundered Lamas.

"And how do you propose I do that against a ghost? No, wait, you said there were two now. You didn't hire a ghost buster," quipped Grant.

"I think closing the lab was the prudent thing to do for the holiday weekend. Not many tourists would be in there anyway, plus it gives your people a chance to enjoy this holiday. I'd suggest just having someone come in briefly each day to check on the readings of the buoys, and leave it at that," said Commander Oslo.

Grant and Lamas didn't respond. They had been arguing back and forth for the last thirty minutes. Commander Oslo had arrived and explained what had happened to young Bradley at the base. Luckily, none of the coins had been taken. Sara, Tim and Becky were in the meeting, as was the commander and the kid, Bradley, who timidly raised his hand to speak.

"What is it, Seaman?" asked Commander Oslo.

"Sir, it seems to me that we have nothing to worry about as far as the base goes. That first mist I saw went away as soon as the other one arrived. I don't think that it will come back. And that second mist, it arrived a good thirty seconds before any security arrived. So if it wanted to kill me or make me vanish, it could have. That second mist just seemed different. It didn't *feel* evil like the first one. I think it will stay away from the coins in the safe. I believe you could then concentrate our resources on protecting boaters and divers that get too close to the treasure."

"Why do you think that?" asked Commander Oslo.

The youngster shrugged. "Whatever that first mist was, it wasn't after me. It could have made me vanish, but it pretty much ignored me and went for the coins. It only came at me after I hit the base alarm. The thing seemed nervous, like it wanted to get the coins and just leave."

Becky nodded her head and spoke up. "It makes sense. Didn't Captain Ross tell Teller he'd protect military people from his evil spirit just after Teller said he'd haunt the Straits? If so, the second mist could have been the ghost of Captain Ross, fulfilling his duty to the military."

Archie Lamas shook his head. His face turned a deep red, and he looked like he was about to have a stroke.

"I can't believe all of us are adults and are talking like this and actually believing it."

"I thought you had come around," quipped Sara.

Archie shrugged. "I did too, then I didn't, I keep going back and forth on this. Anyway, none of this is really our primary concern. It's Friday morning, and already if you take a look out there you'll see many more boats out there. By late afternoon and early evening these waters will be filled with them. Not to mention divers who want to see the *Voyager.* Even after the fourth is over our season will be much busier. We have to pay attention to the safety of all those people out there!"

"We will. I have two cutters out there. We also have five civilian boats that are being contracted to keep an eye on things. I can't see anything else we can do unless you want to close the

Straits to all boating, which of course the governor will never do," said Commander Oslo.

"Since Tim and I won't be working, we'll take a boat out and help," put in Becky suddenly.

Tim turned a surprised look toward Becky. She was actually including him in her activities now, not trying to go it alone. Was this the opening he'd hoped for? Was her armor starting to crack and let him in? Tim smiled inwardly. He would still take it slow and easy with her. No more sudden moves.

"That's right, I'll be happy to help out. It will be helpful for the coast guard to have every pair of eyes out there possible," agreed Tim.

"I'll stay on shore, and hang out in the lab. I'll monitor the buoys. I'll have a radio so I can contact you two. Just let me know what channel you'll be on," put in Lamas.

"And I will be with Sara, helping her out, not that I want to be on all that wet stuff out there," said Steve. The others laughed at the remark.

"You all look like you've got it covered. I'll stay on the island, playing tourist. But I'll keep a radio, so you can get in touch with me if need be. I'm there for all of you. I'll give all my support and expertise to both groups as you go out. Don't worry, you won't be alone. I'll be readily available," said Lamas

"He's there for us. I feel safer already," said Tim in a mocking whisper.

Becky did her best to maintain a straight face, but she finally laughed and then pushed him in the arm, playfully, for cracking her up when everyone was being so serious.

* * *

The semi-truck slowed down, and finally came to a complete stop. The driver stepped out, went to the back and pulled open the heavy doors as the impatient owners watched.

"Come on, come on! We don't have all day!" thundered Steele. The driver cast an annoyed glance at him before approaching.

"You want to unload this? Otherwise shut up and stay out of my way!" Steele took a couple steps back from the big man, clearly intimidated. Ellison and Billy had no desire to challenge the man either. Carl merely shrugged and suggested he do what the man asked.

A ramp slid out the back, and a trailer pulled up to the end of it. A long sleek tube slid out the back of the truck and eased its way to the trailer. It was a new submarine to replace the one they had lost. But this one was better, much better. It was longer, heavier, and more technically advanced. It also had a special design Steele had insisted on, a tube for firing spears similar to those fired from a spear gun. He even had some spears modified so they had explosive heads, making them basically small torpedoes. He wanted to make sure he could shoot back this time if something came after them.

"If you move your truck and attach the trailer to that jeep, we'll pay you double what you were getting. In fact I'll do even better. We need this sub put in the water at Mackinaw City. It's only two miles away. Tow the sub there and get it in the water for us, and I'll triple your fee,' said Ellison. The man's eyes got large. Assholes or not, he couldn't pass up that kind of money for maybe thirty more minutes of work.

"You have cash on you?" he asked. Billy pulled open a briefcase full of cash. The man grinned. Even the briefcase was very good looking. It appeared that it was made of real leather.

"One little condition, and then I'll agree."

"What's that?" asked Carl.

"I get to keep that nice leather briefcase."

Steele rolled his eyes while Billy just laughed. "Yes, of course," said Steele.

"Then you guys have a deal."

* * *

The boating traffic was heavy, too heavy. The spirit didn't like it. It was time to move the gold again. He needed to find some place where all these people wouldn't think to look. He wasn't about to lose any more coins than he already had.

He hadn't given up on the gold on land. He would get it back sooner or later, and those who had it would pay dearly. The other one that watched out for the military people wouldn't stop him next time. He wouldn't stop him from getting what was rightfully his. But all in good time. For he had time on his side. In fact he had all eternity to get the rest of his gold.

But for now, he had to again hide the chest. Soon the gold was in just three feet of water near the back of Round Island. There was even a red buoy there, which would serve as a marker for the chest. Nobody would think to look for it in water that shallow.

Chapter 10

Buoy 101, northeast of Round Island, conditions: Air Temperature: 82 degrees F, water temperature 61 degrees F. Sea conditions: waves 3-5 feet. Winds from northwest at 8-12 knots, gusts 15-20 knots.

The day before the fourth of July was perfect, and the fair weather was predicted to last the entire three-day weekend. A few cumulus clouds drifted lazily by. The temperature was in the low eighties. If there were any complaints, it was from people using sailboats who would have preferred to have a bit more wind. But even they grudgingly consented that the weather was adequate.

Becky and Tim approached the lab's cabin cruiser that had been provided for them to help patrol the busy Friday waters. The lab was closed down for the weekend, except for a few scientists who had agreed to come in over the weekend and check the readings recorded by the buoys. As they approached the dock, they saw Steve Grant and Sara approach and prepare to board the second and final lab boat.

As usual, Steve was unhappy. "I can't believe they are making me go out in all this wet stuff! I'll get even one day, I promise you that! Geeze they know what I feel about the water and evil ghosts and stuff."

Steve was cut off as Tim roared with laughter. "You're gonna kill yourself with worry boss. You need to relax. Besides, Sara will take care of you and fight your battles for you," he said, trying to stop laughing.

"Tim's right, I'll take care of you. You're safe with me," said Sara with a wink.

"I sure hope so," he mumbled.

"We'll be on channel twenty-nine if you need us," put in Becky.

Sara nodded. "We'll stay on that channel too then. Good luck to all of us. I hope things are peaceful and relaxing for us all out there," said Sara. "It's a lovely day for a boat ride."

A few seconds later Archie Lamas arrived, seemingly agitated. His face was deep red, like it was sunburned. He was waving his arms around, and nearly lost his grip on the expensive radio he was carrying.

"Having a bad day?" asked Sara innocently. Archie shot her a sour look, but ignored the remark. He walked straight to where Becky and Tim were preparing to board the boat.

"Why aren't you all out in the water yet?" he stomped his foot impatiently as he spoke.

"We're going, just take it easy.   If you're so concerned you should be going out too," said Becky, her voice edged with distain.

'Watch your tone, Vasquez, it sounds insubordinate to me," warned Archie.

Becky just shrugged. "I didn't think that civilians had anything like that."

"Yes we do. We can't send you to prison for it like they can in the military, but I can still fire you for it."

Becky gave him her sweetest smile. "So sorry, sir. If you don't mind then, we'll be on our way," she said. Lamas tried to detect sarcasm in her voice, knowing that was a sarcastic remark, but really couldn't detect any. She'd disguised it too well. With nothing to really hammer her on further, he settled for shooting her a dirty look.

"Fine, just get going."

"Of course, sir, if there is nothing else?" asked Becky sweetly.

Without waiting for a reply Becky hopped into the boat while Tim began to undo the lines of the boat. Lamas in the meantime motioned for Sara to join him. She sighed and got out of the boat.

"I thought you were in such a hurry for us to leave?"

"I am. But first things first. Don't you think Vasquez is getting a bit, uppity? She was so kind and respectful when she started the job. Now she's really pushing the envelope a bit with her behavior," complained Lamas.

Sara sighed. "Look, she's finally starting to find herself. When she first came here, her attitude wasn't really her. She'd been through an extremely traumatic event in El Salvador. And it just ate her up inside. Her normal way is to be fiery and brash. We are just starting to see that come out in her. That's a good thing." Archie sighed, looked at the water and sighed again.

"How do you know all this? She's said nothing to me."

Sara shrugged. "We talk fairly often. It took a while, but she finally trusts me enough to open up to me. She's beginning to trust Tim too. Things are finally turning around for her. Please sir, I know you're the boss. She does too. And she does respect you for that, whether she shows it or not. But just cut her a little slack. I'll make sure she doesn't get too out of hand, okay? And Tim is having a positive effect on her too."

"Okay, okay. I get it. I trust your judgment. So tell me, are she and Tim having a romance?"

"Not really. They're friends. Tim's doing most of the pursuing. Becky's been somewhat resistant. But again, she's starting to bend a little."

"I see. Okay, well, get going then. I'll do what you ask, Sara, out of respect for you," assured Lamas.

"Thank you, sir." Sara climbed into the boat and shortly they were on their way into the straits, followed closely by Becky and Tim. The radio crackled for attention as both boats cleared the nearby-automated beacon.

"Becky, Tim, head south about a mile, then swing east, toward Round and Bois Blanc Island. We'll swing west toward the bridge and the Lake Michigan side." It was Sara's voice.

"Copy that, on our way," responded Becky.

* * *

The sub was finally in the water, and Billy, Steele and Ellison were pleased. This was a much better, more advanced sub than the one that had gotten wrecked. It had some weapons also, so they could fight back if necessary against anyone, or anything.

Carl took his usual place at the controls and began to nose the sub downward. Billy kept watch with the periscope. He had been keeping a close eye on Becky and Tim, and now that they had boarded a boat, they intended to follow them with the sub. Steele was convinced they knew where the chest was, and intended to use the boat to go and get it.

Carl shook his head. "I really doubt that. They are helping the coast guard keep an eye on the boaters this holiday weekend, that's all. I doubt very much they'll do anything but take the boat around to keep any eye out for trouble."

"Look, something of theirs was taken to the coast guard station. And something unusual happened there according to this reporter I bribed. But the coast guard is being very closed-mouthed about it. That in itself is not right. They know where the coins are, and we'll follow them everywhere they go. Eventually they will go back to where they are," said Steele confidently.

"But what if that ghost-spirit thing moved the chest again? It always seems to. Then they wouldn't have any more idea where the gold is then anyone," put in Billy. Steele shrugged.

"Even if that is true, I'm totally convinced it was some of the coins they locked up at the base. So they somehow got coins away from that thing. So eventually the coast guard will return the coins to her. And when they do, we'll be there to take them from her!" laughed Thomas. Billy shook his head.

"It won't be as easy as you think. My jaw still hurts from where she kicked me."

"Let her try and kick bullets away!" Billy swallowed and turned away. Again he was afraid he was in way over his head. What would he do if things came to a showdown? Would he actually be able to hurt Becky? Billy didn't know if that was in him or not. But at the same time, he couldn't very well let his new friends down. There were plenty of other women out there for him to tame. He figured he'd cross that bridge when he got to it. If things went okay, maybe it wouldn't even come to a showdown.

* * *

Austin Thomas was having a great time.   Here he was fifty-one years old, and he had a blonde twenty-three-year-old girlfriend. What a life he had. It was just plain perfect.

He stood up in waist deep water just a little northwest of Round Island. Most of the other boaters and divers were farther west in the straits, so they had plenty of privacy. He spotted his girlfriend slowly making her way from shore to the water. She was preparing to snorkel with him, and was currently fixing her mask and air hose.

Austin used to lust after her in the recent past. But now, he wanted more. She was everything he'd ever wanted in a woman except for one minor problem, she was a typical blonde bimbo. If he could only get her to accept some professional tutors, she'd be perfect. He still considered himself lucky to have her, and he'd probably never dump her. But he hoped one day she'd take up the offer of some more education so that he could at least have intelligent conversations with her.

A couple boats zipped by him, hardly more than a hundred feet away. Large waves kicked up and completely washed over him, making him slip and fall into the water. Austin got up and angrily shook the water off, while shaking his fist at the rapidly receding boats.

I wonder if anyone on those boats is sober, he thought to himself. He took a glance at shore and saw Vicky come into the water. Suddenly all animosity was gone in an instant.

Vicky took an experimental step into the water and quickly pulled her foot out. Geeze the water was cold here! Here it was the third of July and the water was still like ice. She much preferred the expeditions they'd had into the tropical areas of the world. She tugged on the bottom portion of her one-piece red swimsuit down farther around her legs. No need to show Austin everything so soon. When they got back to the Grand Hotel that evening she could show him all he wanted and more. Tonight would just be an appetizer however, tomorrow, the Fourth of July would be the *real* deal. Vicky smiled. *Tomorrow night we will make our own fireworks! Tonight, the evening before the Fourth, we'll just set off a few sparklers.* Until then, he'd just have to control his animal instincts.

Vicky stepped back into the water and gritted her teeth, trying to fight off the cold water. She could see Austin snorkeling not more than fifty feet ahead of her. The cold water didn't seem to bother him at all. She sighed and walked back out of the water and sat on the beach. She loved Austin despite his advanced age, but he was changing in a way she wasn't sure of.

He'd had several conversations with her recently about taking some night classes or online courses. He felt she needed to make herself a bit more aware of the world. She scoffed slightly to herself. That was just his nice way of saying she was kind of stupid, a dumb blonde. Well, so what if that was true? She knew important things like how to keep herself beautiful. And wasn't that enough? Of course it was! She would make sure that Austin realized that too.

Austin waded in and took her hand.

"Come on Vick, let's snorkel a little farther out. You'll get used to the cold water fast enough." She hesitated, and then finally took his hand. They walked out together into deeper water.

"What about sharks? That scares me," said Vicky, looking around as she spoke.

Austin shook his head vigorously. "There is nothing to worry about. There are no sharks in the Great Lakes."

"How do you know that? You know my friend, Jessica Sexton? She told me just last week that she and her boyfriend saw a fin break the water, and they got a real good look at the rest of it too!"

Austin rolled his eyes and sighed. "Where were they when they saw it? And who is her boyfriend, what does he do?"

It's Joel Griseous, you met him last summer. He works with the chamber of commerce, to promote tourism and stuff. Isn't that scary? They saw it near Petoskey, not far from the big state beach there."

"Joel is just trying to drum up tourism, that's all. There are not any sharks in any of the Great Lakes. They are salt-water animals, and the lakes are fresh water. They couldn't survive."

Undeterred, Vicky pressed on. "I thought he said it was a kind that could live in fresh water, I think he called it a cow shark or something."

Austin stifled a laugh. "I think he said a Bull shark. It's true they can live in fresh water. However, they are still tropical animals that prefer warmer water. If one did get into one of the lakes they'd quickly realize how cold the water was and look for the quickest way back out."

This seemed to satisfy Vicky so she agreed to snorkel in deeper water. They did so for the next hour, and Vicky had to admit it was fun. She forgot all about sharks and thoroughly enjoyed the experience.

When the hour was up, she swam closer to shore and stood up where the water was about shoulder depth. She began to shiver.

"Austin, I'm getting cold. I'm going in to get a towel."

"Okay, Vick. I'm going to keep going a little longer."

"No problem. No hurry. Take your time."

She began to wade slowly back to shore, shivering the entire way. She noticed her skin turning purple. *Now that's cold,* she told herself.

* * *

It had been an uneventful, rather boring day for Becky and Tim. They had gone every direction of the compass, keeping a wary eye. They had seen two cutters out also, and met other private boats that were providing security. It had gone well, nothing had happened by noon that day before the fourth.

Tim was presently grilling hamburgers and hotdogs on a grill he'd brought out with them. Becky sniffed with appreciation at the aroma. She was also impressed with Tim's attitude. He finally seemed ready for anything that might crop up on them. He'd been very alert, and was constantly scanning the water with binoculars. He had a level of confidence that she hadn't seen in him before.

Becky wasn't sure how she knew, but she just knew that if something happened, he'd be there to back her up. He wouldn't back down like he had in the past. It made Becky's resolve not to get involved with Tim melt even farther. She knew now that he had captured her heart. Was she ready for a serious relationship? Tim had made it clear that was what he wanted. The fact that he'd been willing to wait for her to feel the same way made her love him even more.

"Burgers and hotdogs are ready, Becky," announced Tim. Becky got up and eagerly began preparing the food. They were currently at anchor, about two hundred yards west of the Round Island buoy, in about eighty feet of water.

As they ate, Tim looked behind the boat and frowned. He looked again, and squinted slightly.

"You're going to think I'm nuts, but I think there is a periscope watching us," said Tim.

Becky laughed. "I know. It's been following us around all day. My guess is that Steele, Ellison and Billy have gotten a new sub. They are keeping a close eye on us, thinking we may be going to where the chest might be."

"How could we know where it is? It's probably been moved by that thing under the water," said Tim.

Becky nodded in agreement. "Almost certainly it has been. But they know we found some coins, so they may be thinking we know where there are more of them," said Becky casually.

Tim pulled out a nautical chart and looked over toward Round Island.

"There is a shoal not far from Round Island. I say we lead them there, make a quick ninety-degree turn and let them run aground.

Becky laughed. "I like the way you think, Tim!" She jumped up and bounded into his arms and kissed him hard on the mouth. Tim was flabbergasted. His mouth hung open in surprise as the kiss ended.

"Does this mean I'm making progress?" he asked.

Becky smiled. "Yes you are. I am finally beginning to trust you, Tim, and I pray that my trust isn't misplaced. I don't think I could handle another betrayal, and certainly not from you."

"I know that. But I won't let you down. I am finally learning what it means not to back down or get jelly legs when things get tough. I'm learning that from you. And I can guarantee you I will never let you down," said Tim with more conviction than Becky had ever heard.

"And for the first time, I don't doubt you at all. Keep doing what you're doing and you and I have a real chance at a long relationship. But remember, what happened to me is still in my mind. I have baggage that I bring to the table," responded Becky. Tim shrugged as if it were no consequence.

"Who doesn't come with baggage? We all have it. Trust me, Becky, having baggage just proves you're human and you had a life before you met me."

Becky just smiled in response.

* * *

Vicky sat on shore and wrapped the big towel tightly around her. The sun warmed her enough to pull the towel off. She got up and walked to the edge of the water, looking for Austin. He had just stood up in nearly shoulder depth water, and was slowly making his way toward the shore. Vicky marveled that he could handle the cold water for so long.

She was preparing to speak to him when a flash of light caught her eye. Then it flashed a second and third time. Confused, she looked around for the source, and finally saw something under the water. It was just off shore, maybe two or three inches under the water. It appeared to be a gold coin of some kind. It was glittering on and off as waves passed over it.

Vicky waded into the water, suddenly forgetting how cold it was. She reached down and plucked the coin from the water. It looked old, and looked real. It had an eagle on one side, and the words *United States of America,* engraved above the eagle. On the other side was a man, but she wasn't sure who it was. Below the person was a date, *1800.*

Vicky was so engrossed at looking at the coin, she didn't see Austin arrive from deeper water. Seeing her look at something he put a hand on her shoulder, and looked over it.

Vicky went ballistic, jumping two feet up, and nearly out of her bathing suit. Some kind of gold object flew out of her hand and plunked into the water. Austin grinned. *Now that would be something to see, her jumping out of the bathing suit,* he thought.

Vicky glared at him, holding her chest.

"Don't sneak up on me like that!"

Austin looked apologetic. "Sorry, I didn't mean to scare you…I was just wondering what you were looking at."

"It was a coin, and it looked old too. Damn it, where did it go now?" She began to look for it in the water while Austin stood and watched. She shot him an irritated look.

"Since it's your fault I dropped it, you could help me look ya know."

"Oh, yes of course. Sorry, Vicky. I'll make it up to you tonight okay?" He snuggled close to her and kissed her neck. She blushed slightly and nodded.

"Okay, now help me look."

"Sure." It only took a few seconds for Austin to see the coin shimmer under the glassy-clear water. He scooped down and picked it up. He turned it over and over, carefully studying both sides of the coin. He let out a long whistle, and a big smile crossed his lips. Then it was replaced by a frown. Austin looked around, seemingly nervous about something.

Vicky looked around, confused. She saw nothing but water, trees on the island, and a few boats nearby. She saw nothing that would worry her.

"Something wrong, Austin?" Austin nodded.

"We need to get out of here, *now!*" He took the coin and tossed it to the sandy beach. "Leave it," he added.

"Why? I want it…" began Vicky.

Austin cut her off with a wave of his hand. "Let me tell you a quick story…" He began to tell her of the event of 1801. She listened intently, but seemed unconvinced at the end.

"Aren't you the one who told me just a little while ago not to believe in things, like sharks in these waters? This seems like just a story to scare people with at night when it's dark. I may not be the smartest girl around, but I know there aren't any ghosts or curses and stuff. And it seems to me boaters disappear all the time. It's not a big deal. I'm taking that coin. It could be very valuable if it's that old. Maybe I could trade it in for a new summer wardrobe."

Austin could only sigh. Her mind was made up. She picked the coin off the beach and brushed away the sand.

"Come on, let's go. We'll be safe in the Grand even if there is something to the story."

Austin could only nod. "Okay, I suppose that's right. But I still don't feel good about all this. Something just doesn't feel right."

Vicky waved his concerns off. "You're just paranoid because of the story and the curse and all. A lot of people and boats have disappeared here too. It's just stories," said a confident Vicky.

Austin could only nod in silence and hope she was right.

* * *

Another one of its coins was in danger. It wasn't happy, and he would never allow that to happen. The mist seemed to hover over the chest. Yes, it was fine. Now to deal with the mortals. The spirit floated toward the boat that was just leaving with its coin.

No, another boat was too close, and it seemed to have a military presence on it. The mist turned from blue to crimson red in anger. It floated higher in the sky and faded until it looked like just another cloud. It could watch the boat that took its coin, see where it went, and then it could strike that evening when the mortals were unprepared.

* * *

After finishing lunch, Tim took a casual look behind the boat, as if he was just looking at other boats. Yes, the periscope was still there. He grinned to himself. Good, now they could have a little fun. Tim spoke to Becky, who warned him to look casual, so they wouldn't cause any suspicion. It was obvious they could watch their movements on the boat.

"Just pretend we are studying a map, then we'll head for the shoal near Round Island. Hopefully they'll run aground, then we will get the laugh at their expense,' said Becky. Tim nodded, and pulled out a nautical chart, and the twosome pretended to study it. With a nod of satisfaction, Tim put it away while Becky took control of the boat. In a slow arc she turned the boat eastward toward the southern shore of Round Island. The sub continued to follow at a discreet distance, and showed no signs that it would stop following them anytime soon.

Becky headed the boat away from the island, and then made an abrupt turn toward the island, all the while increasing the boat's speed. She wanted to make it look like they had suddenly found something of interest.

Whoever was driving the sub seemed to be caught by surprise, and it dropped further and further behind. As they speeded toward the island the periscope got larger and larger. They were catching up.

"About time. I thought I'd have to slow down for a minute there," observed Becky. Tim laughed and gave a casual look toward the rear of the boat.

The periscope was very close now, even within the wake of the boat. They were obviously determined not to get too far behind again. That was perfect. Becky eased the boat forward, and took a quick look at the chart. The shoal was just a few yards further up. She had to make sure she turned away in time, otherwise they'd be the ones stuck. Becky gunned the engine, and the boat lurched forward. The sub responded instantly and also lurched forward. At the last second Becky turned slightly to the left, and killed the boat's engine. The sub was unable to imitate the act, and lurched forward, striking the shoal. Becky and Tim heard a gratifying sound of metal grinding against the gravel of the shoal.

"Great job, Becky! That'll teach the rich asses a few things about us locals!" Tim ran to the rear of the boat and yelled out, as if the occupants in the sub could hear him.

"Ha! Who's the dumb peasant now? That's right, we are the man, and the lady!" Becky shared an amused look with Tim, who had a very satisfied look on his face as he walked back toward the pilothouse of the boat.

They moved away from Round Island, and noticed an expensive speedboat pull away. Behind the boat was a bluish fog, moving closer and closer.

"Do you think that's it?" began Tim. Becky responded by gunning the engines. They approached the speedboat and the fog suddenly evaporated. The occupants in the boat, an older man and a young woman seemed surprised at their sudden arrival. They gave a welcoming wave. Tim returned the wave as Becky pulled alongside.

"Hello there, how are you today?" called out Becky.

The man called back. "We are fine. How can we help you?"

"We are assisting the coast guard this holiday weekend, just checking with various boaters, making sure everything's okay," finished Becky.

"I see, well, we are fine as you can see. We just finished snorkeling, and now we are headed back to Mackinac Island. We need to get rested up before the fourth tomorrow, lots of plans."

"Okay, think safety first with boating and all your activities," said Becky.

The man nodded. "No problem, we will. We don't expect to become statistics."

Becky and Tim bid them farewell, and watched as they continued on to the island. "What do you think? Did they find any gold?" asked Tim.

"Hard to guess. They certainly didn't see the mist. They were far too calm. Maybe we didn't either. I only got a glimpse of something."

Tim nodded. "Yeah, me too."

* * *

Vicky watched as the lab boat slowly moved off.

"So why didn't you tell them about the coin we found?" she asked.

"I just didn't want to. It's not that I didn't trust them, but gold can do things to people sometimes, make them a little crazy. Besides, it was just one coin. It's not like we found the entire chest or something. It's ours, we found it. Nobody else needs to know," said Austin.

Then he fixed his gaze into Vicky's eyes. "Do you understand that? Nobody is to know about this until we decide to sell or trade the coin or whatever."

Vicky swallowed, and slowly nodded. This wasn't a part of Austin she'd seen before. He just seemed so obsessed with the coin suddenly. Why a few moments ago he had wanted to just leave it on the beach. Maybe he was right and gold *did* do some strange things to people.

* * *

The metal of the sub shrieked as though in pain as it struck the rough shoal near Round Island. The threesome inside lurched forward as the sub came to a sudden halt. Steele's head smacked hard against the metal bulkhead. He cursed loudly and put his hand against a rapidly expanding welt on his head.

"What the hell just happened?" he thundered. Ellison shrugged helplessly, unable to meet his withering gaze.

"We ran aground on a shoal, that's--"

"I know what a dammed shoal is! What I want to know is how the hell did this happen?"

Ellison turned a deep shade of red. He was getting tired of Thomas Steele's attitude. He never did anything, except yell at him when things went wrong. Steele thought that since he made more money than he did he was the big boss. Well, since they were supposed to be friends, neither of them should be a boss. They should agree together on things, not just whatever happened to pop into Steele's peewee brain at the moment.

"I was busy watching them through the periscope, and I couldn't watch the sonar at the same time," said Carl defensively.

"Well then Billy you should have been watching the sonar! We are bringing you along for the ride you know. You could do a little work here!"

"Now just a second--" began Billy, but was cut off by Carl.

"Back off, Thomas, all you do is whine all the time. You never help out any way, shape or form. You just holler at us when things don't go the way you want. If you helped out we wouldn't be in this mess. So just back off!" thundered Carl.

Steele crossed his arms and looked away, clearly incensed by their current situation, but unsure what to say or do now. It did no good to alienate his buddies here, and he did need their help to get the chest, and somehow stay away from the curse. He figured he'd better start mending a few fences now before things really got out of control.

"Okay, okay. I get it. Let's not get all pissy here. We all want that gold right? If we don't work together we'll just end up as numbers in a newspaper or something," said Steele, his voice much more reasonable sounding.

"I'm for that," put in Billy quickly. Trying to get the group once again focused on finding the gold.

"Yeah. It's okay. Now if you'll excuse me I will try to reverse the engines so we can get off this shoal," said Ellison.

It took about fifteen minutes of going forward, then reversing, but finally they were able to free themselves.

"Where to? Mackinac Island?" asked Carl.

Steele shook his head. "No, let's head back to Mackinaw City for now. We can have some brunch. We know where those two are, we'll deal with them and the damage they've done to our sub soon enough!"

* * *

By late afternoon, their safety patrol was finished. They received word from Lamas to return to the island. It had been a quiet day, with no incidents to report. As Becky and Tim pulled into the marina near the Mackinac Island visitor center, they saw Sara and Steven arriving also. As they tied off the boat, they saw a wobbly Steve get off, with Sara holding on to his arm. She wore a big grin, while Steve just looked plain miserable.

"That jerk Lamas, making me go out into all that wet stuff! I'm lucky I can still breath. I about hyperventilated out there. Thirty minutes is my limit on water and he damn well knows it! He and I are gonna have to have a talk on how to treat people."

He steadied himself against Sara and made it successfully off the dock without falling in, all the while threatening to sue Lamas if he did.

"Looks like you had fun," laughed Becky.

"Oh, yes, Steven Grant is a riot. He complained the entire time out there," responded Sara.

"I've got a right to, dammit! Now y'all leave me alone. I'm going to my room and try to calm down." He walked off followed by thunderous laughter from the others.

"You guys are finished for the day. If you like you can go home if you want. I'm going to go hit my apartment myself I think and try to relax some," said Sara, waving as she walked away.

"I guess that just leaves us then. Want to do anything? Or just catch the next ferry back to Mackinaw City?" asked Becky.

"Actually I got myself a room at the Huron Inn. It's a double room suite with a hot tub. I've got it for tonight, and the fifth. I also have a room booked in Petoskey for the fourth. I want to break up the routine a little. I got a double room for a reason though." Tim smiled and watched her expectantly.

Becky tensed. "Okay, you say they're double rooms, so there is actually a door between the two rooms that locks, right?" asked Becky.

Tim nodded. "Yep, it sure does. See? That makes you totally safe. Besides, if I did try something you didn't like I know you'd kick my skinny butt all around the room," said Tim.

"You have a skinny butt?"

Tim shrugged. "Yeah, mostly I think. You could take me up on the offer and find out."

Becky chuckled at his teasing, but then turned serious again. "Tell you what, Tim. I'll spend the night with you. It could be fun. But I'm not saying I'm going to *spend* the night with you, okay? As long as you understand that."

Tim nodded. "Of course. I totally understand. That's why I got double rooms," replied Tim, his cheeks getting slightly warm. "I really didn't intend for us to actually spend the night together, just, well, you know, more or less hang out together."

"That suits me. Just remember if you try anything I don't like, you may end up flying through the window."

Tim laughed. "I wouldn't want that."

* * *

Evening on Mackinac Island was magical. The lights came on, casting a soft, cheery glow around the small city. The hustle and bustle of the day died down, and the sounds become as muted as the lighting. Only the occasional clip-clopping of horses, intermixed with a few soft-spoken voices could be heard.

It was no different for Austin and Vicky out away from the town, enjoying the seclusion of the Grand Hotel. The twosome sat on a long couch at the front of the hotel, enjoying the peace and quiet. A large fountain in front of them shot water up in the air, adding soul-soothing tranquility to the scene.

Vicky closed her eyes and tried to think about nothing. All she wanted to do was soak up the stillness of the evening and nothing else. But Austin was making that increasingly difficult for her to do. He still had the coin. In fact, he hadn't let it out of his sight or even out of his hand. She was amazed she'd been able to talk him into coming out on the porch at all.

Presently, he was sitting on the porch flipping the coin from front to back, front to back, looking at it time and time again. It occurred to Vicky that he was indeed becoming obsessed with it, and was determined to try and find the rest of the coins. She wondered how the coin changed him so quickly into a person that she couldn't recognize. She didn't like this side of him at all. It made her feel very uneasy inside. She wished that she'd never found the coin at all.

A few passersby's called a cordial greeting. Austin shoved the coin in his pocket, and shot an annoyed look at the people.

"What do you want? Do we know you?" he snapped rudely. The people looked surprised at his reaction, but said nothing. They moved along as quickly as requested.

"What's gotten in to you? Why are you being so rotten? I don't like this side of you much," said Vicky.

"If they see this coin, they might figure where we got it and go look for the chest themselves. And I found it, it's *mine!*"

"*I* found it," corrected Vicky. "And I wish I hadn't now," she added quickly.

"We should go in now. It's getting late." Austin looked over at Vicky and saw the pained, almost frightened look on her face. He seemed to snap back to reality. He sighed, finally realizing that he had been acting very rude and obnoxious the past several hours. It hurt him more than he could say to see the look on Vicky's face. He put out his hand and rubbed her back, smiling.

"Let's go up to our room. I'm sure I can make it worth your while," he said with a wink.

Vicky smiled. Now *this* was the Austin she liked. "Okay, looks like there is a fog coming anyway, look." She pointed toward the edge of the water far below them.

Austin looked and could plainly see what appeared to be a bluish gray fog beginning to come ashore. Funny, it almost looked like a person. Then suddenly he felt afraid. He remembered stories he'd heard about a bluish fog making boats in the area disappear. He grabbed Vicky's arm and began to tug on it.

"Come on, let's get to our room and lock ourselves in for the night."

* * *

The fog slide easily onto the shore, unnoticed. It was evening and not many mortals were around. It transformed itself into a typical mortal person and looked up a large hill where the long white hotel sat. Its senses clearly told it that the coin was there. Good, it wouldn't be long before it was back with him where it belonged.

* * *

Austin turned the coin over and over, still looking at it. Somehow Vicky had managed to get his shirt off, but could get no further, as he again became obsessed with the coin. Vicky had in the meantime stripped to her underwear, but now sighed as she sat on the bed waiting for Austin. She was very no longer in the mood for sex, and was getting angry.

"Maybe I'll just slip this underwear off and walk down the hall and offer my services to someone else. I'm sure I could get some takers, what do you think?"

Austin looked up from the coin with an absent stare and only nodded his head, then he turned back to the coin again. "Sure, whatever you want babe."

Vicky was furious. She hastily pulled her clothes on and kicked the wall, stubbing her toe. She let out a tirade of curses while massaging the injury. Austin finally looked up and paid attention, attracted by the sudden commotion.

"What's going on? How did you hurt yourself?" he asked innocently.

"I hurt myself kicking the damned wall! How the hell do you think? If you'd pay attention to me and not that coin, all evening maybe you'd notice a few things!"

Austin set the coin down and sighed.

"Sorry again. Guess it just has some kind of power over me. I did tell you that gold could do funny things to a person. I guess that I'm no exception. Tomorrow we should go back out to the area and try to find the chest."

"Yeah, yeah. Whatever you want. We might as well go to bed. I'm not in the mood for anything else tonight."

Austin shrugged. "Tomorrow night it will be the best ever, I promise. The Fourth of July will be the best night that we have ever spent together."

Vicky just rolled her eyes. *Yeah sure. You can't even take your eyes off that one coin. What will happen if you find more?* she wondered.

* * *

This was almost too easy. The ghostly form had transformed itself to one of the motel employees and walked easily though the area. No one even seemed to notice him at all. Only a few quick glances were turned his way as he walked slowly by. Obviously the mortals were too busy with their own tasks to care about him. His eyes glowed a brighter and brighter red as he got closer and closer to the gold. Yes, it was just up the steps. The spirit glided up the stairs and looked down the hallway. Yes it was three doors down. It came to the proper door and converted back to its bluish mist, and was inside the room in seconds.

Austin and Vicky had not yet turned the lights off. They both sat stunned as the mist came in the room. It was bluish, with red glowing eyes. It looked like a blue person. The form changed and it became more solid, even more like a regular person, save the red, glowing eyes.

Vicky screamed in horrified terror. She threw herself to the far side of the room, cowering.

Austin stood up slowly and faced it, a look on his face as evil as that of the spirit.

"I know who and what you are. You want this." Austin showed him the coin.

"Austin, are you crazy? Let him have it, please! Let's try to run!" Vicky was crying and screaming at the same time.

"No. We can't run. This thing will never let us go. We have what it wants." Austin felt strangely calm. He had no fear at all. It was prepared for the inevitable, but he'd still fight till it happened.

The spirit raised its arm and extended it.

"I will take my coin now. Then you will go to the other place." The thing's voice was cold, heartless, devoid of anything that might resemble humanity.

Austin found himself suddenly paralyzed. He struggled, but couldn't move despite his best efforts.

This was too much for Vicky. She ran out on the balcony, screaming for help. People in the hallway were alarmed by the scream and hurried to the room. The door was open. Three people arrived, and two promptly disappeared, vanishing into thin air. The third person stumbled backward into the hallway, unable to believe what he was seeing.

* * *

Becky and Tim decided it was a perfect night for a walk before heading to their suite for the night. Tim figured the walk should be something of a challenge so they decided to walk up the long hill leading up to the Grand Hotel. The view at night from up on the hill ought to be spectacular. They weren't disappointed in the least. The streetlights leading up to the hotel were placed in the middle of the street and cast an inviting glow the entire way up the long road. A few other people walked by nearly all waving to them and saying good evening.

Of course, neither Becky nor Tim knew any of them personally, that was just the way things were on Mackinac Island, friendly and relaxed. People came here to get away from the stresses and the daily grind of their usual lives. Here on the island that sort of thing just melted away, and it seemed everyone could sense that.

It occurred to Becky and Tim that if people acted in the same small town way, wherever they lived, the world would be a much better place. But then, that was why both of them wanted to work here in the first place, the stress free environment. Of course the events going on in the straits didn't exactly keep things stress free, but what the heck, they both needed just a little adventure this summer anyway.

About ten minutes later they reached the summit of the hill, and were as close as they could get to the Grand without actually staying in the hotel. Anyone else wanting to go on the massive porch had to pay a ten-dollar fee to do so. It wasn't because the place was snobbish and didn't want "common" people there, not at all. It was just the way the hotel was able to maintain its grand traditions and protect the privacy of the guests.

They were turning to look out upon the darkening straits when they heard the screaming. The woman they saw on the boat near Round Island came out on the balcony of her room on the third floor. She was yelling hysterically and waving her arms.

"Help, someone help! We are being attacked by a ghost!"

Becky and Tim looked at each other, stunned. Could it be these two had found some coins? It had to be true.

"Come on!" shouted Becky, hurrying the rest of the way to the motel lobby.

"I'm with you. But what are we going to do when we get to the room?' asked Tim, running to keep up with her.

"I guess we'll wing it and see what happens," replied Becky between bouts of sucking in air as she ran.

"Okay, let's wing it then. That's what we do best anyway."

* * *

The deep waters of Lake Huron spawned the second spirit, the one who had saved the young coastguardsman. It sensed that a military person could be in danger, and that it would not allow. It exited the water and glided easily to the shore. Its supernatural eyes blazed red, but a softer, much less harsh version than the other one. Its senses told it exactly where to go, and it wasted no time in getting there.

* * *

Becky and Tim, plus about four other people arrived just in time to see a grim drama take place. The woman was still on the balcony, screams intermixed with sobs. Inside the room the ghostly arms of the spirit seemed to touch the man. He jerked as if suddenly shocked. Lights seemed to flash. Then, incredibly, he vanished.

"No! Get away from them!" Becky screamed and entered the room. The spirit turned and gazed directly into Becky's eyes. She stared directly back into his. Tim tried to move forward to assist, but Becky put a restraining hand out.

"Stay there." She turned back to the spirit and locked her eyes directly into what she thought were its eyes.

"I know who you are now," said Becky in a barely audible voice. The ghost seemed to hesitate ever so slightly in its move forward. Then it suddenly jerked around and glided quickly out the balcony window, ignoring Vicky as it passed over her. The others entered the room and looked out the window.

"Look, another one!" A man pointed as another mist seemed to approach at rapid speed. It chased the other mist, then stopped as it vanished in the water far below. The other ghostly figured approached the balcony as Becky walked out and stared at it. Its red eyes seemed to soften as it looked at her. Becky felt a sense of calm. There was no terror and fear from this spirit. It looked at her a moment longer, its glowing orbs locked onto hers.

Becky smiled slightly. "Captain Ross," she murmured. The spirit's eyes flashed red briefly on and off, and then began to float away. "Thank you!" called out Becky. The mist stopped, and seemed to look at her for another moment, then continued to float away until it was out of sight.

Tim walked in and stood next to Becky. "Boy could this story hurt tourism," he joked.

Becky smiled briefly, then faced Tim and gave him a long kiss on the mouth. "That's for not running out on me a moment ago."

Mackinac Triangle

Chapter 11

Tourists jammed the island tight. All events were going on as planned, and nothing appeared to be out of the ordinary. This year's Fourth of July celebration was proving to be the best ever.

Behind the scenes things were much different. The mayor of Mackinac Island, Harold Andrews, nearly had to be sedated. The local state police were ushered in to do some serious damage control. And every person who saw or was even near the incident was sworn to secrecy. The last thing anyone wanted was to scare off the tourists, not only for this particular day, but also for the rest of the summer. There was a briefing for those employees who witnessed the attack, and they were told only to say it was a domestic dispute.

Mayor Andrews then called a meeting with Commander Oslo, Sara, Lamas, Grant, Becky and Tim. To this point the mayor had pretty much stayed out of the picture as far as the disappearances went. After all, they had only occurred in the waters around the island, not on the land itself. Until now. He had no authority over the waters surrounding his island, but he did need to protect the mainland.

"Come on, I need answers and I need them now!"

Commander Oslo threw up his hands in frustration. "If this is a ghost or spirit, how exactly are you supposed to stop it? That's not something the Pentagon trains us in," said Commander Oslo.

Mayor Andrew looked even more enraged and turned to Lamas. "Surely you and your scientists can come up with something."

Lamas could only mimic the moves by Commander Oslo. "I must say, Mister Mayor, I am at a loss. For the longest time I refused to believe this thing even existed. I am just now coming around to the fact that it does. But now that I, and all the rest of us, do believe, the next step is to somehow stop the thing. But, I mean, how do you stop a ghost?"

The mayor got up and stormed around the room, pacing out his frustration.

"Okay then, today is the Fourth of July. Can we protect all these tourists that are here?"

Becky decided to put her two cents in. "The only time it makes people or boats disappear is when they get too close to the gold. Had Austin not found that coin, he would still be with us, not in some other dimension. So I think unless someone comes near it they'll be okay," said Becky. The others all chimed in to agree.

"What about that woman, Vicky?" asked the mayor.

"Vicky was spared because as we arrived the other spirit showed up and…"

Becky suddenly stopped speaking, and got up. She walked slowly across the room, thinking.

"What is it?" asked Tim. Becky looked at Tim, then the others. She seemed to hesitate, then responded.

"I know now that evil spirit is Teller."

"You mean Lieutenant Teller, the one that tried to steal the fort payroll in 1800?" asked Mayor Andrews.

"1801," corrected Becky. The mayor looked annoyed.

"So how does that help us," he asked.

Sara snapped her fingers and spoke up. "I think I know what Becky is driving at. You're thinking about the other spirit that showed up are aren't you?"

Becky only slowly nodded her head. "It's the same one that showed up when the young coast guard seaman was being attacked. Is that what you think?" asked Lamas.

"Yes, I do. It's Captain Ross. He was protecting me like he did the young coast guard member."

"So he won't allow certain people to vanish? He'll can stop Teller?" asked Tim.

"Yes," said Becky, her gaze drifting again.

"It makes sense. When Teller had his final words before he was executed, he told about cursing the gold and so on. At that time Ross reportedly told him he'd never allow Teller to curse them," said Sara.

"Geeze! I'm gonna stick next to Becky then! I don't need no monsters after me!" piped up Grant.

"So then you coast guard people and you Mrs. Vasquez are the key to defeating this thing!" said the mayor.

Becky responded in a grave tone. "How? Even if that part of the story is true, all it means is that we can't vanish. But it doesn't help us defeat the thing."

"This meeting is a total waste of time. We have lots of tourists waiting to get into the lab for tours, and our scientists, Sara included, have work to do!" exploded Lamas suddenly.

"So what are you going to do?" asked the mayor incredulously.

"We are going back to work in the lab, while the coast guard does its thing in the water. Isn't that right, Commander Oslo?" asked Lamas.

The commander nodded his head. "Yes. I see no point in beating a dead horse."

As they exited the conference center and headed to the lab, Tim and Becky ran into Billy, Ellison and Steele. The three stepped directly in front of them, effectively blocking their way.

"If you value your life and want to keep your man-parts intact, I suggest you step aside," said Becky calmly.

Billy swallowed hard. He'd seen this before, and he had no desire to be on the receiving end of her wrath again. He began to move, but was restrained by Steele.

"You damaged our sub by running us up on that shoal near Round Island. I demand you pay for the damages!" He thundered.

Tim shot him an innocent look. "We have never been on your sub. I, we, have no idea what you are talking about," responded Tim.

"Somehow you knew," said Ellison.

"Knew what? This is boring me. We both need to get to work. Tim has already told you we have no idea what you are talking about. Now get out of the way and let us pass," said Becky, the calmness leaving her voice.

"Fine, you win this time, but trust me, we will be around," said Steele. The threesome walked off as Becky and Tim continued to the lab.

They had been in the lab about fifteen minutes when the rest of their coworkers walked in. They looked tired and frustrated. It was obvious that they hadn't gotten anywhere with the mayor.

Sara approached them a few minutes later. "Just take this upcoming group, then you can go for the day, and the two of you can enjoy the forth," said Sara.

"Thanks--" began Becky.

Sara waved it off. "Don't mention it. Well, if you'll excuse me, I better get back to work, and it looks like we got a nice group ready to come in," said Sara, pointing at the door.

With a sigh, Tim opened the door and the group nearly knocked him over in their haste to get in. They followed the normal procedures as Tim moved a scanner over the group. As he did so, Becky gave her standard speech on the history of the lab and the lakes, and her normal warning not to bother the scientists as they worked.

At the end of the tour Becky handed out replica coins to everyone. They were exact copies of the ones that were in the chest on the *Voyager*, and would have been the payroll for the fort soldiers and their families. Happy with their souvenirs, the tourists exited the lab.

Soon afterward, Tim and Becky hopped a ferry for Mackinaw City. From there they drove thirty-five miles south to the city of Petoskey. They both felt good to be getting out of the straits for a while.

There were several events at Petoskey's waterfront that day. A fast pitch softball tournament, several bands playing live music, and various food grilling and barbeques. Of course that evening the city would host the traditional fireworks, with the bands playing patriotic music while they were set off. Also, several boats from the waterfront marina would be out in the bay, firing off fireworks also. It would be quite a sight to see the water nearly explode as fireworks were launched from several boats, at the same time the main city display was being launched.

During the day they sat, watched softball games and ate hotdogs. It was a glorious day, one they would remember for a long time. For Tim, he hoped this would be the first of many of the holidays they'd spend together. Tim had the presence of mind to bring two sack chairs with them, which was perfect. They faced them toward Little Traverse Bay, but were still able to watch the games.

"You know, Becky, I should really thank you. Without people like you having real courage, willing to go through things like you did in El Salvador, we wouldn't be able to sit and have all this fun today."

Becky smiled and reached out, squeezing Tim's hand. "You're very welcome. I appreciate you saying that. But you're really thanking the wrong veteran. The ones we should really be thankful for were the ones in the Revolutionary War. The ones at Lexington, Bunker Hill, Valley Forge and Yorktown. *They* are the ones who made this day possible." Becky shook her head and got that faraway look on her face again.

"I can see where you are coming from, but without people like you maintaining what they did, we'd all be screwed."

Becky laughed and hugged Tim tightly, then proceeded to kiss him long and deep.

Tim held her tightly after the kiss was over, nuzzling her ear. Becky smiled, enjoying the feeling. Her senses were telling her Tim was a better man in a way Billy never could have been. Hopefully, the changes she'd seen in Tim recently were for real, not some made up act to get her to fall for him. Well, with the events going on near the straits, if he were faking it, it wouldn't take long for her to find out.

Evening came all too quickly, and more boats from the marina headed into the waters of Little Traverse Bay. There were several miniature explosions and fireworks began to fire off several boats in the bay. That in itself was quite a sight, but a few minutes later the city display began. The bands played patriotic music, and the scene was complete.

To Becky, this had to be one of the best fourths she'd ever had. She felt overcome with happiness. For the first time since El Salvador, she was ready to live, and love again. She surprised even herself by grabbing Tim and kissing him long and hard, then clutching him tight.

She suppressed the small part of her that still wondered if Tim would betray her like Billy. He had changed. He hadn't backed down at the Grand Hotel. Calmness returned to Becky as she looked into his eyes.

They left a few minutes later and went to their motel rooms. Soon, Tim heard a soft knock on the adjourning door and hurried to open it. Becky stood there, smiling and confident. Smiling back, Tim reached out to draw her nearer. "Are you sure," he said softly.

Nodding, she tilted her head and kissed him.

Reassured by her response, he deepened the kiss and reached to skim his hand down her backside. Pressing her against himself, he backed up, pulling her with him.

Lifting his head, he said, "Last chance to change your mind."

Taking his hand, she pulled him to the bed and tugged his shirt over his head. "Nope, no turning back now."

He eagerly agreed, pulling his arms out of his sleeves and tossing his shirt onto a nearby chair. Hers soon joined it, and he reached to unfasten her bra as he recaptured her lips in an intimate kiss.

The rest of their clothes soon followed the first, and they moved onto the bed to consummate their deepening commitment to one another.

* * *

Steele and Ellison laughed at Billy's reaction as they entered the motel room, fully armed. They weren't about to let these two out of their sight, even for a day. They knew where the gold was, and at some point they would go and get it. And when they did they'd have the rifles ready to take it away from them.

"There is no reason to stay here. Come on, let's go. I don't want to hang around here," Billy complained.

Steele laughed. "You're just pissed that Tim took your woman from you."

"Now just a damn minute there...!"

"It sure looks that way from this end," said Ellison, slightly more sympathetic sounding.

"Yeah, so what? It's that way for now maybe. But just wait till we show up with our weapons after they find the gold. He'll pee his pants, and Becky will see what a fake he is. Then she'll still come back to me,' said Billy with more confidence than he felt.

"And if she doesn't?" asked Steele.

"Then Timmy will pay dearly for stealing my woman away," spit out Billy with fresh venom.

Chapter 12

Becky thrashed in her sleep, and whipped a leg out from the covers, as if she was kicking someone.

Tim woke up immediately and tried to wake her, only to get her arm thrust into his chest. He gasped, but was undeterred. "Becky, wake up, it's okay, no one is after you now. You're in a motel room with me, safe."

Becky sat up with a start and looked around the room. "I was having a dream. I have it sometimes…"

"It's okay, don't worry about it. I understand," assured Tim.

Drawing her close, he convinced her that he meant every word.

Becky and Tim were up early the next morning, despite their late night, and got a head start on getting back to Mackinaw City. They were both curious to see if there were any incidents while they were gone.

Despite their mutual enjoyment of the previous night, or perhaps because of it, the morning was somewhat awkward for them. Tim couldn't look at Becky without blushing, which Becky thought just showed the respect he had for her.

They drove north in a somewhat awkward silence, so Becky figured it was time to break it. "Are you okay? You don't regret last night do you?" she asked.

"Heavens no! That was going to be my line. It was wonderful, showing my love for you like that. I was a little scared about what you might be feeling, that maybe you would regret it."

Becky squeezed his leg and smiled. "Not at all. I trust you like no man I've ever known, including, no, make that especially Billy. I hope you understand what else happened last night. As you can see I come with baggage. I could very well have these dreams the rest of my life. It's not too late for you to back out on me. And if you do, I will understand. But…I hope you won't."

Tim just snorted, shook his head and returned the leg squeeze with his free hand. "We all come with baggage. And I do understand. So you'll have these dreams at times. So what? I'll be there to take care of you when you do."

Becky released a relaxed sigh and smiled, while Tim inhaled a relaxing breath. Now they could determine exactly where this relationship would take them in the future.

* * *

The spirit hovered over the chest by Round Island. It was still in the same place, in just four feet of water a few yards from shore. The specter hesitated, unsure whether to move it or not. Finally it decided to leave it. The mortals would assume he would move it again, so he'd leave it safe in the same place. It melted easily into the water and became part of the bottom of Lake Huron.

* * *

Becky and Tim arrived at Mackinaw City and hopped the first ferry they could to the island.

158

When they arrived at the lab, they saw Sara, wearing shorts, lying out front in a lawn chair soaking up the sun. She seemed to be in a good mood, greeting them warmly.

"Well, it's good to know things are normal for at least a little while," said Tim. Sara nodded, but looked slightly grimmer.

"But we need to try and stop this curse thing, somehow. There must be some way. Otherwise there will always be the constant threat of that thing out there," said Sara.

Neither Becky nor Tim could help being downcast about this comment, but they also knew she was right. They had to stop the thing, and soon. The question was, how? The only way to even get it to appear was to stumble on the chest, which obviously some had done, or they wouldn't have disappeared. But even that appeared to be blind luck. Becky could only shake her head in frustration trying to think of a way to beat the thing. She wondered if perhaps there was some way to use the other spirit, the one she was certain was Captain Ross to combat it, and finally defeat it.

"We have some company," said Tim, pointed down Main Street.

Billy, Carl and Thomas approached them with the usual sneers on their faces. "We're going to come to the point. We want that damned gold and we're tired of chasing you all over this place for it. So just save us some time and tell us where the chest is. We have some new weapons on the sub, so we can get the chest safely. Just tell us so we can all get on with our lives," said Billy, almost in a pleading tone.

All Becky could do was sigh.

Tim shook his head and folded his arms. "I'm going to tell you this, so listen up. We don't know where the chest is. So just stop following us around, and stop threatening us. Have we found some of the coins from the chest? Maybe, maybe not. That's none of your damned business. So take your sub and go look. Maybe you'll get lucky and find it. Maybe you'll find it and somehow remain in this dimension, but I doubt it. Mortal weapons won't work against this thing," said Becky.

"I'm tired of this whole thing!" shouted Steele. He reached out and grabbed Tim's shirt. "Tell me where the chest is!"

Tim remained outwardly calm, but he reached up, grabbed two of Steele's fingers, peeled them away from his shirt, got them in a hold and bent them back, quickly. The man instantly released his hold on Tim's shirt and cried out in pain.

"Don't ever put your hands on me again," Tim said softly, bending the older man's fingers back until he had brought him to his knees.

"Okay, okay, let me go!" cried Steele.

"Yes, please, let him go so I can break him in half," offered Becky. Tim used his free hand to gently pull her against his side.

"I can handle this," he said briefly.

Becky smiled and just nodded.

"Well, don't think I'm above striking a woman. In fact, either tell me where the chest is or I'll just beat it out of her, since you don't want to cooperate."

Billy looked horrified at the exchange. He stepped forward and said, "Let him go," trying to pull Steele away from Tim.

Tim released his finger hold and allowed Tim to tug Stelle's arm and pull him to his feet.

"I don't think this is a good idea…" Billy began, but was cut off by Ellison.

"Just stand back then. If you don't have the stomach for this, watch those who do," snarled Carl, apparently angry at the turn of events.

Steele, enraged at Tim's treatment of him, nodded at Carl and the two of them suddenly lunged at Becky.

Becky pulled away from Tim and stepped aside. Steele missed with a closed fist punch. She backhanded him across the side of his head, sending him dazed to the ground. As Carl dodged around Steele, Becky caught him directly in the face with a kick. He went down hard, blood spurting from his mouth.

Tim's mouth was agape at the speed with which she'd dispatched the twosome. He hadn't gotten a chance to do anything. So he turned to Billy, ready to do what he'd been wanting to do all weekend.

But Billy wanted nothing to do with either of them. "Hey, I told them not to start anything, and you heard me." He threw his hands up in surrender, backing away from Tim's angry glare.

With that many tourists around, it was no surprise when the local state police arrived. They took statements, and finally asked Becky and Tim if they wanted to press charges for assault.

"Look at us! We are the ones bleeding. *They* assaulted *us*," said Ellison.

"They defended themselves against an unprovoked attack by you two," corrected one of the state policemen.

"When you pick a fight, you better make sure the woman you attack isn't so capable," stated the other. Several of the bystanders started to laugh. Becky spoke briefly to Tim who nodded.

"It's okay officer. We think they've learned their lesson. We won't press charges," announced Becky.

The state policeman shrugged. "Okay, have it your way. As for you three, stay away from these two, or next time you'll be locked up whether they press charges or not, for public nuisance and disturbing the peace."

* * *

Evening approached and the sky turned a navy blue. It was a view that Todd and Chuck never got tired of looking at. As usual, they were the sober, designated pilots of the yacht, while the other fifteen people on board were having a post Fourth of July, Saturday night party. Todd grinned and shook his head. Not that they needed it, but any excuse to drink, they did.

Chuck joined him on the top deck near the pilothouse.

"The party is in full swing now. The others were sober enough to say they'd like to stay by Round Island, so they'd like us to drop anchor. We'll have to keep an eye on them though, we don't need any drunks trying to jump off the yacht and wade to Round Island. They'd end up drowning in their condition," laughed Chuck. Todd returned the laugh.

"Okay, we'll keep an eye on them. For now, let's go below and relax a little." He dropped the anchor and the twosome made their way below to the whooping and hollering below deck.

* * *

Back on Mackinac Island, Becky and Tim walked along the beach near the wooden boardwalk. It was quiet this evening, and the twosome were enjoying some relative solitude. They sat down on a pebble-strewed beach and looked across the straits. A good-sized yacht sat at anchor near Round Island.

"Hope that chest isn't still there. They could be in trouble," commented Tim. Becky nodded absently while straining to hear. She grinned.

"Well, if they do get in trouble, they'll probably never know it. Listen carefully. I doubt there are many sober people on that boat," said Becky. Tim strained and could hear the partying going on in the yacht.

"Well, it sounds like they are having fun," commented Tim, chuckling.

* * *

The spirit was alert. Something was near his gold, more mortals. They weren't acting like mortals normally did though. It was making the ghost uneasy, unsure how to proceed. But as usual the greed of the ghost overruled any misgivings, and it headed quickly for its gold.

* * *

On the yacht, the top deck was indeed full of people having a lot of fun. They drank, danced, played loud music and generally made total fools of themselves.

A young lady near the railing at the back of the yacht was the first person to see the strange looking fog approach across the water. She cocked her head to the side and looked curiously at it. She felt no fear at all.

She turned to a male near her and called to him.

"Hal, bring another brew over here, we got another guy joining us!" The man looked over and saw the figure for the first time. The others on deck began to notice it one by one. All began to move to the rear of the boat to greet the newcomer.

"Here you are my funny looking blue friend. Have a beer." Hal held out the bottle and tossed it at the funny looking bluish person. It seemed to fall through him.

"Aw, he didn't catch it, get him another!" called out the young lady.

"You betcha." Hal grabbed another bottle. "Hold out those big arms of yours, this should be easy to catch!"

"Foolish mortals! I will make you go away for being by my gold, you'll vanish to the other place for all eternity!" The young lady and Hal, along with the others on deck dropped the beers they were holding and covered their ears.

"Whoa there dude, not so loud. That hurts my ears. Or I guess it could be the beer making your voice so loud," said Hal.

The others just laughed, "Yeah, it's the beer talking alright."

The ghost hesitated. It didn't know why the mortals were acting like this, with no fear and such childish playfulness. It wasn't sure if it could make these mortals vanish. It needed their terror. It fed on it. But these mortals didn't show any of this at all. It decided it had to try. They were far too close to his gold, and no one could be allowed to be near his gold.

Attracted by the loud voices on deck, Chuck and Todd popped on deck and immediately realized what was happening.

"Holy…" began Chuck, but was cut off by Todd.

"I don't think so."

Chuck pointed to the pilothouse of the yacht. "Sneak up there real easy like, retract the anchor and get us the hell out of here. And do it slow and easy, the last thing we need to do is piss off that thing. I'll go below and use the radio to call the coast guard, or anybody that will listen."

Todd nodded and began to half crawl up the short steps to the pilothouse. He used the people on deck as a shield, hoping the ghost wouldn't see him. He made it successfully and began pulling the anchor up. Once that was accomplished, he took the yacht in a slow arc away from the area toward Mackinac Island. A few glances behind him showed the ghost wasn't following him.

Below deck, Chuck watched the water slowly pass by, and something caught his eye. He pulled out binoculars and clearly saw the brown chest below the clear, yet now darkening waters.

No wonder it appeared. We were close to the gold! Chuck made a mental note of where he had seen the chest. It must have been only in three or four feet of water. Afraid of attracting attention, he decided to wait until morning to report the incident and the chest. They appeared safe for now. The ghost wasn't following them. *Of course not, the bastard just wants to keep that chest protected,* he thought. Well, he could have it!

* * *

Back on shore, Tim's eyes blazed with fire when he saw the fog appear. The yacht then began to slowly leave the area. Tim shook Becky who had fallen asleep on the beach and pointed out to Round Island. Becky was quickly alert. She saw the fog floating and the yacht leaving.

"I wonder why they didn't vanish? They must be pretty close to the chest for the thing to show up," murmured Tim.

"Well, they are leaving the area. Perhaps they realized what was going on in time. Hopefully nobody on the boat will vanish," said Becky.

Tim's eyes lit up. "Hey, we know where the thing is. We can get out there now and finally fight the thing, end this once and for all!"

Becky shook her head. "No, it's getting too dark. But I like your attitude. We'll wait till morning, and then we'll have the others from the lab and the coast guard with us. There is strength in numbers."

"But won't it move the chest? It won't show up if the chest isn't there," said Tim.

Becky nodded. "It will show up.' She pulled out one of the gold coins. "I've kept this with me, waiting for the chance to get that thing to come to me for a final battle. Tomorrow is that day. We end this tomorrow. Either it goes away forever, or we do."

Chapter 13

Todd and Chuck reported the incident to Archie Lamas in the morning, and Chuck mentioned where he'd seen the chest. Commander Oslo was there, as were Sara, Grant, Becky and Tim.

Becky confirmed that she and Tim had seen part of the incident also.

"Okay so now what? How does this help us?" asked Lamas. Becky stood up and spoke forcefully.

"This ends today. Tim and I are going out to Round Island. If the ghost of Teller has moved the chest, I'll pull out one of the coins I kept when I turned the rest over to the coast guard," said Becky, with an apologetic look at Commander Oslo, who only grinned and shook his head as though not surprised.

"That should get him to show up. Then Tim and I will fight him. Like I said, this can't go on any longer. We have to stop this thing. Today it's gone for good, or we will be. If that's the case, then I guess it will be your problem," stated Becky.

Lamas looked furious, his face a deep red. "Who put you in charge? All you do is give tours!"

"We are going, now." Becky got up, and was joined by Tim.

"Leave this room and you're fired! You'll go nowhere. I forbid it!" thundered Lamas.

"Shut up! They are doing what needs to be done, since you haven't the guts. I have to approve any firings and I don't. And I'm going too," said Sara firmly. Lamas looked helplessly around the room for support, but wasn't getting any. All he could do was throw his arms up in frustration. He looked over at Commander Oslo who only gave him a dismissive shrug.

"Becky has a point. I'd allow her to continue," said the commander.

"Fine, then so be it. Grant, since members of the lab are going and you're responsible for their safety, you must go too!" said Lamas. Grant threw his arms up.

"Oh sure, thanks! I hate the water, and I hate monsters! So fine, I'll go. But if I disappear, I'll never speak to any of you ever again!"

"What about you commander?" asked Sara. He shook his head.

"I will not put a cutter and the entire crew in danger. But I could go myself, and my first officer could be put in charge in case something happened," said Commander Oslo.

Becky shook her head. "Sir, you're needed too much in the area. You should not be placed in any danger. Let me, Tim, Sara and Grant handle this. Unless Mr. Lamas you're coming too?"

Lamas looked uneasily around the room before replying. "No, as director of the lab, I'm too important. I'll stay here. But I will watch and monitor the situation from here. Just radio me, and I'll provide you with leadership, from a discreet distance of course."

"Of course from a safe distance," said Sara, rolling her eyes.

"So how do we fight the thing when it does show up?" asked Tim.

Becky shrugged, and got up from her seat. "I have no idea. I'm planning this as we go along."

* * *

The spirit was angry, very angry. It turned from bluish to a crimson red. The chest was safe for now, but mortals were trying to steal it and some of the thieves had gotten away. That was not an acceptable situation. Suddenly its attention was diverted elsewhere. Mortals were on the way here, several of them. So, it was the female mortal, the one who knew who he was. Good, very good. This one had been a nuisance long enough. He could finally rid himself of her once and for all.

But, she was military. That could pose a problem. The ghost would need to use his other assets to defeat her. He didn't think he'd ever need these assets, but at this point he knew he would need them. No problem. He would call them when he needed them.

* * *

Steele, Ellison and Billy watched as the large group walked to the boat and prepared to cast off. As far as Steele and Ellison were concerned, they had no intention or just staying away, regardless of what the police had said. Billy wasn't at all happy with following them anymore, but he had nowhere else to go and these two were paying his expenses for everything, so he decided to stick around.

"I knew it! I'll bet they are headed to Round Island. That's where the gold is!" exclaimed Steele.

"But that means the ghost will be there too!" said a worried Ellison.

Steele brushed the protest off. "No problem. While they are occupied trying to be heroes fighting the ghost, we'll just sneak in behind and take the chest."

Both Ellison and Billy agreed it was a good plan.

"Of course it is. Now, let's follow at a very discreet distance, and then we can come duck behind the island and come around and snatch the chest. They'll be too busy fighting the ghost to be able to stop us, and the ghost will be too busy making them vanish to see us. We'll be in and out before they even know we were there."

* * *

After taking a deep breath, Becky began to cast off the lines. She wasn't nearly as relaxed as she pretended to be, but didn't want to show it. She had no desire to vanish to wherever in the hell people who had disappeared were now. And it probably was a place in hell they were going to. She was young and figured that she still had a lot of living to do yet. Perhaps she and Tim even had a long, bright future ahead of them. At least she hoped they did.

She felt confident she and Tim would win, somehow. She had been spared in El Salvador for a reason. The Lord could have taken her then if he had chosen to. But He didn't. Her experiences recently had made her think more about religion and God. Truthfully, she really hadn't given either subject much thought in the past. Instead she relied on herself to take care of situations.

But now it began to dawn on her that there might be another force out there that could be assisting her, and helping her out in certain situations. Her senses were so in tuned with her surroundings, it was almost like she was physic. She didn't have those skills by accident that was for sure. Somehow she was given those skills. If she made it through the next few hours alive, she promised herself it was time to visit the inside of a church again.

"Are we ready to go?" asked Tim. Becky took another deep breath and nodded.

"Yes, let's get this over with." Tim swallowed hard at Becky's grave sounding tone, but continued to unhitch the boat from the dock. In a few minutes they were heading out to Round Island.

* * *

Billy, Thomas and Carl stayed behind. The other boat showed no signs that they had seen them. It seemed like they were absorbed with what they were doing, and weren't bothering to look behind. They seemed to be expecting the ghost to show up, which clearly indicated either they knew where the chest was, or they had some coins on them. Either way this played directly into their hands. They could sneak in and steal the chest before they knew it was gone.

"Get ready to go to the rear of the island. We'll come around the backside. Then we'll wait along the south side. We'll have a clear view of everything, and when we get the chance we'll rush forward and grab the chest," instructed Steele. Nodding silently, Carl steered the boat as he had been told, while Billy settled for looking like a very nervous young man.

* * *

About fifteen minutes later they arrived at the location Todd and Chuck had stated they had seen the chest. Other than the dread they all felt, it was a glorious day. The lake conditions were even calm, with the waves generally between one and two feet. Sara and Grant looked on the beach to see if any other coins might have washed up, while Becky and Tim scanned in the water a few feet off shore.

Sara's radio crackled. "This is Lamas, are you four in position?" Sara rolled her eyes.

"Yeah, we're here. Nothing has happened yet, but just keep the mike open, it could at any point. It would be best if you just listened in to what was going on. Don't call us. We're libel to get real busy here soon."

"It's essential that I know all that it going on for your safety," stated Lamas.

"If you're really worried about us, come on out here and really support us," stated Sara flatly.

"I'm too valuable to the lab to risk being lost. I'll have to support you from here. There is no other way."

"Well if that's all you have to say then I need to go. We have things to do here."

"Fine, but keep that damned radio up, I want to know what is going on at all costs, I mean that now too!"

"You're scary when you sound tough," laughed Sara. The others grinned. They could almost see Lamas fuming back at the lab, nice and safe.

About ten minutes later Tim shouted and pointed behind where they had been looking for the chest. They could clearly see something under the clear water about four feet down. As they all waded out, it became clear that it was the chest. Grant reluctantly picked it up and carried it to shore.

Of course he wasn't happy about this at all, and wanted to leave the chest and hurry away. But even he knew that there was no turning back now. All of their eyes lit up, even Grant's, when they opened it. It was still mostly full of the payroll that never got delivered that fateful day in 1801.

Becky dropped the coins she was holding and stood up slowly.

"We have company," she breathed. She walked away from the chest, and the others followed. About a hundred yards ahead of them they could see the blue mist approaching at rapid speed.

"This is it," said Becky simply.

* * *

"They've done it! They found it!" exclaimed Billy as he looked through binoculars. Steele grabbed another pair and watched intently. He was right. They had found it.

"That's not all they found, look what is approaching them," reported Carl. The threesome could clearly see the mist approaching.

"Perfect. Get ready. When they start to try and fight that thing we run in and grab the chest, and then we're out of here richer than ever," said Steele.

* * *

Becky stood, forcing herself to remain calm. She breathed easily and closed her eyes, taking in the sounds of nature. A smile came across her face, which seemed to go blank, with a faraway look on it.

"Sara, Steve stay back about fifty feet," said Becky.

"Hey, no problem! I could even stay back farther if you like…" he was cut off by a hasty jab in the ribs by Sara.

"Sorry, just being honest," he mumbled.

"What should I do?" asked Tim.

"Stay next to me unless I tell you otherwise."

Tim swallowed hard and nodded, trying to slow his currently racing heart. "Okay, I'm here, and ready."

The ghost arrived shortly, hovering over all of them. It looked like a thirty-foot blue person. Eventually it changed. It became smaller and suddenly materialized just ten feet from Becky. It looked like a real person now, wearing the uniform of the American army in 1801.

It took another step toward Becky, then froze.

"Trying to steal my gold!" The voice from the ghost thundered. It seemed to fly off the ground, and turned back to the thirty-foot fog. It flew away from Becky and the others, totally ignoring them now.

Confused, Becky turned around, as did Tim and Sara and Steve. They soon saw the reason why. Steele, Ellison and Billy had snuck in behind and were trying to get to the chest.

Becky ran toward them, waving her arms and yelling. "No, you fools! Go, get out of here! Leave the chest!"

It was to no avail. Billy dropped the chest and ran in terror to the wooded area of the island, cowering behind some trees. Both Steele and Ellison refused to give ground, and began firing at the ghost with shotguns. The shots seemed to pass though the spirit, causing it no harm. The arms extended out and wrapped around both of them. They continued to fire shot after shot into the foggy ghost. Then abruptly, both of them vanished. The ghost floated away from the scene, stopping to pick up the chest and set it gently near the edge of the water.

Billy stayed hidden in the trees, with the spirit showing no inclination to go after him. It then returned to where it had been standing originally, and was soon the same person, one about five foot nine wearing an American army uniform from 1801.

This time it was Becky who took the step forward.

"So you are Lieutenant Teller?" asked Becky.

The spirit nodded. "I am. So you know the truth." The voice of the Lieutenant bordered on reckless arrogance, like it felt totally unstoppable.

"Why don't you take off that uniform? Materialize into something else. You're nothing but a dirty traitor to your country. You don't deserve to wear the uniform of your nation's military!" Becky thundered back.

Teller was genuinely taken aback by Becky's courage and hesitated before replying. But it wasn't long before it found its arrogant voice.

"I wear what I please. You are nothing but a foolish mortal, and a foolish female who bowed to military authority. You are a weak-minded, foolish woman."

Becky had had enough and sprang into action. She lashed out with a series of kicks and punches that would have felled a normal person, male or female. But this wasn't any normal person. It was an evil spirit of the past. Her attacks merely passed through him.

The specter laughed, an evil, horrifying laugh.

"You fool! No mortal attacks will affect me!" Something like a blue laser zapped from its right index finger, hitting Becky squarely in the chest. She was knocked back at least fifteen feet. Smoke rose from her chest, the aroma of burned flesh floated in the air.

"No!" wailed Tim. He ran over to Becky, who wasn't moving, then interposed himself between her and Teller.

"I won't let you hurt her again! Come on, fight me, fight a man! Not a woman, you coward," challenged Tim. Tim rose to his feet ready to do everything in his power to protect Becky. He felt a restraining hand pull on his arm. It was Becky. She struggled to her feet and managed to stand on her own. A second later her strength seemed to rush back.

"Stay back Tim, this is between me and him. There isn't anything you can do."

"But--"

"Do what I say Tim. I know what I'm doing. There's nothing you can do, you *can't* defeat him, now go! Get over by Sara and Steve." Tim looked from Teller to Becky and slowly nodded his head, and then silently moved over to where the others were waiting.

"Brave young one, but a waste of your life. Now you will go to the other place."

"No dirty traitor can stop me," she hissed.

"Oh, but they can. You see, evil is more powerful…"

Teller never got the words out. Another thirty-foot ghost appeared and landed next to Becky. Its form changed like Teller's had. It was Captain Ross, still wearing his uniform. Becky smiled. *Am I glad he finally showed up! I was fresh out of ideas!* she thought.

"This is over, traitor Teller. I told you that you would never be able to hurt any military person. And now it is time that you once again are gone forever. You will no longer hunt any mortals. Part of the gold was yours, but you forfeited that when you turned traitor to your country."

"Captain Ross, you cannot put me in front of the firing squad again. My powers are superior to yours, and I have allies. You have none, as you will now find out!"

Teller waved his arms and there was an explosion of water. Two canoes full of ghostly Iroquois Indians and pirates surfaced and quickly made their way to shore. In a matter of moments Becky, Ross, Tim, Grant and Sara were completely surrounded by at least fifteen Indians and pirates.

"Now, you will surrender to us, and will go to the other place. Do not resist Captain. Your eternity need not be totally unpleasant," said Teller in a mocking tone.

Captain Ross looked around and saw he was completely surrounded, but looked unimpressed. In fact, he looked calm.

"Whatever you need, I'm with you to the end captain," said Becky. Captain Ross looked at Becky and nodded.

"Thank you for your offer of assistance, but it won't be needed." Captain Ross stepped forward until he was just a few feet from Teller.

"You forget some very important points. Your source is that of evil. My strength comes from the light, and that pure source is always more powerful. It has given me the ability to finally end you. You will become mortal again, will face another firing squad, and this time, you will stay in Hell where you belong!"

Teller backed up a few feet, looking suddenly uneasy. Even the Indians and pirates began to waver. A few even vanished.

"Do not go! He can't make us mortal by himself. He would need many others to do this! We still have victory within our grasp!" shouted Teller.

"That is correct of course. But do you really think I would come and not bring the help I needed to finally end you? I have all the help I need. Take a look to the water in the west."

All attention turned west in time to see a churning of water. A whirlpool was forming on Lake Huron, followed by a brief waterspout. When it ended, water shot up like a geyser. A second later a ship appeared. A real ship. Becky smiled. She had seen that ship before. She and Tim and many others had dove to it. It was the *Voyager*.

It sailed to their position, and twenty American troops piled off and began to surround the Indians and pirates. They had results in seconds. Several vanished, leaving only a few behind. Those who were left looked around, and apparently considered that the odds were no longer in their favor. They vanished shortly thereafter.

"Cowards! I'll fight myself then…"

"You are now mortal, Teller, as are we all," stated Captain Ross. There were flashes of light, like flash bulbs going off. Teller, Ross the soldiers all changed, and looked totally human, which they now were.

"You will be executed again here and now. Then you will be banished like the fallen one to Hell for all eternity," stated Captain Ross.

"So he's just a regular person now?" asked Becky.

"Yes, as are we," answered Ross.

"You dirty traitor, Teller. What a selfish pig you've been, even killing people after your death because of your selfish greed. You're going to burn in hell for your crimes."

"Says who?" He snarled, shoving her away from him.

Despite the additional pain caused by his hand pushing against the burns on her chest, Becky's training helped her react defensively. She jumped back and lashed Teller with double kicks to his head, sending him dazed to the ground. He tried to get up and fight back, but another kick to his temple put him out for good.

"That's the least you deserve for what you did," said Becky.

Some soldiers hauled Teller to his feet. Though sorely tempted to land a final round-kick to his face, Becky managed to get her anger under control. She smiled as she realized that she was finally on her way to a full recover from the traumatic incidents in her past and no longer felt the need to seek revenge or get even with everyone who wronged her. Yes, she would defend herself if attacked, but she no longer felt the need to lash out at anyone who treated her unfairly or unkindly.

Captain Ross appeared amused by the brief battle. "Are you alright, Ms?"

"Couldn't be better, sir," said Becky, walking to Tim's side and grasping his hand.

The sentence was then carried out again. Only this time, Teller had no final words, and would never again haunt or curse the local waters.

"Now, my men and I will all finally rest in peace," said Captain Ross.

"But why didn't you stop this sooner, I mean…if you had this power?" asked Tim, who walked forward to stand next to Sara and Steve. Even Billy came out of his hiding place to join them, now that Teller had been dispatched.

"The power and decisions were not mine," said Captain Ross.

Without further explanation, he and his men returned to the *Voyager*. The ship began to sparkle red and white. It seemed to disappear, then it moved as a flash of light going straight up until it was out of sight.

As this occurred, more flashes appeared in the sky. They came down from the clouds before stopping on the island and in the water. People and boats materialize from thin air. The young couple that vanished on their wedding night, the Lakes, appeared next to Becky. They were disoriented and frightened, but otherwise unharmed. They noticed all the others around them.

"I seem to recognize those people, yet I don't," said Tom Lake as Jenny pressed close to him.

"Can you tell us what is going on?" she asked.

Becky smiled. "It's a long story, Mrs. Lake."

Chapter 14

There was a lot of fast-talking that occurred the next several days. The coast guard had a lot of damage control to perform. Several people witnessed the incident near Round Island. It was officially called ball lightning showers. Of course the reappearance of many people and boats was a bit more of a problem. It was called some sort of mass hysteria over the years and left at that.

Of course, nobody believed it, and the UFO theories, and government cover-up people had a field day.

For Becky and Tim, they just sat back and rather enjoyed it all. It amused them watching the authorities try to explain away all that happened. Becky recovered quickly from her burns. She and Tim were given a surprise visit by Michigan Governor Jenny Chest, who congratulated them on all they had done.

"I not only congratulate you, but I would also like to offer a job to both of you with my administration in Lansing. I need water czars that go out and make recommendations for the continued wise use and preservation of our Great Lakes. It is vital work for the future, and I can't think of two people that I'd rather trust our water resources with."

"I think I speak for both of us, Governor, when I say we are very honored, and will give this much thought. For now, Tim and I intend to go on vacation for a few weeks," said Becky.

"And that vacation will be in the State of Michigan, anywhere you want. So, any personal plans?"

Becky shrugged. "We'll see. I haven't quite made up my mind about this guy yet, but I have to consider his offer too, to be his wife," said Becky, giving Tim a tight squeeze.

"Well, enjoy yourselves. Any idea where you might go?"

"Some place land-locked, away from water," laughed Tim.

Becky looked up at him and smiled her agreement.

About the Author

Clint was born in Michigan in 1960. He spent twenty years as a medic in the US Air Force, and was lucky to see much of the world. It was those experiences that inspired him to begin writing. Since he loves movies, too, he writes screenplays whenever he gets the bug. Besides writing, he loves weather forecasting, scuba diving, astronomy, Siberian Huskies, and sled dog races. He began writing in 2009 and has written two novels and a screenplay.

Tell-Tale Publishing would like to thank you for your purchase. If you would like to read more fine romance novels, please visit our website at:

www.Tell-TalePublishing.com

www.ingramcontent.com/pod-product-compliance
Lightning Source LLC
Chambersburg PA
CBHW071158180726
48291CB00007B/2502